Briars & Blades

by

Amanda Kaye

To hear about the next exciting release from Amanda Kaye
sign up for her newsletter at
www.amandakayebooks.com/subscribe-now/

1

"You're dead."

Godmother Seven presses the sword to my throat. My back is flat against the woven straw mats covering the training room floor, leaving no room for retreat. Steel bites my skin, and a line of fire races across my neck. Blood mingles with sweat.

She tsks. "Sloppy, Aryanna. You let your body's weakness slow your movements, giving your enemy an edge. How do you expect to fulfill your destiny if you're so easily defeated? Perhaps you need to learn the lesson again." Not a single silver hair has escaped her tight bun, not a single stain on the long green sleeves or skirt of her dress.

I glare at the ceiling, refusing to yield. Heat waves shimmer in the air. My chest heaves against the lavender bodice. Strands of wavy ink-black hair stick to my lips. The godmother smacks the flat of her blade against my cheek; I keep my face frozen, not giving her the satisfaction of a reaction. Bitter iron floods my mouth.

Godmother Seven holds the sword over my face a beat

longer and then steps back. She assumes a starting stance, weapon held loosely by her side.

I scramble up, clumsy from the fatigue dragging at my limbs. My cheeks burn as I scoop my sword from the edge of the mats, then retrieve the dagger from the corner.

Blade upright in front, knife ready in my left hand, I faceoff with the Godmother. Her smirk fuels my anger. I embrace it, using it to energize my muscles. The exhaustion disappears, and my body is feather light as I stare her down. *Let's see how you handle this.*

I leap forward, blade whirling through the air. She sidesteps, bringing her sword up to block. The Godmother turns and swings the knife around, using the movement to slide her blade down mine and flip the sword out of my grip. I release the hilt and drop to the ground, sweeping my foot out.

She hops back. I follow, not giving her time to recover. Kick. Strike. Dart to the side. She grabs my wrist and twists, forcing me to drop the dagger as her foot knocks my legs out from under me.

Godmother Seven rests the sword tip against my stomach. "You combined the *Thressure* and *Bertoni* styles." The grunt passes for a compliment in her mind.

A warmth blossoms in my chest, but I ignore it. Her praise should mean nothing to me. I'm a weapon against our enemies, the tool of their destruction. Being distracted by something so trivial is beneath me. But telling myself what I should feel doesn't stop the pleasure from rushing in. *Ah, burn it, I might as well enjoy it. Anything that gets that Sour Seven's approval is worth celebrating.*

Godmother Three steps into the training room. "It's almost time for her dance lessons—good gracious, she's bleeding!" Her hands fly to her ruddy cheeks.

Seven's flat black eyes never leave me. "She'll heal."

With a last look, Godmother Seven turns away, dismissing me from her mind and existence. She tosses her sword to the floor and stalks out of the room.

The other Godmother kneels and grabs my chin with one hand, tilting my head, examining the thin slice on my neck. "At least this one's shallow. What is she thinking, marking you when any day … Well, go clean up, girl."

With a quick nod, I push myself off the floor and gather up the scattered blades. After hanging the weapons on the wall, I stride out of the room, keeping my steps to a measured pace. Not too slow as to convey relaxation, not too fast to be indecorous.

"Hurry!"

Apparently I misjudged Godmother Three's mood.

The heavy scent of the vines baking in the sun fills the villa, giving the illusion we're stranded in a desert instead of surrounded by lush farms. The heat leaks through the plastered walls as I speed down the shadowy hallways. A sigh of relief escapes me when my small bathing chamber is empty. I quickly strip down and climb inside the waiting hip bath, reaching for the sponge and the harsh bar of soap that always leaves my skin tingling. The lukewarm water is like heaven after the stifling air of the training room.

This month's servant girl slips into the room. Her outfit is at least two sizes too large. It doesn't matter; the Godmothers will dismiss her soon. She carefully averts her eyes as she and sets fresh clothes on the bench next to my discarded outfit.

A strand of black hair escapes my messy bun and flops across my shoulder, the end trailing in the water. I flick it idly while I replay the fight, looking for weaknesses. *There must be a way to defeat Sour Seven. I almost had her with that kick. Mayhap if I follow it with a second one ...* "I'll beat her next time."

The girl squeaks and runs out of the room.

I squeeze the sponge with both hands and mutter, "I wasn't talking to you." I never found out what happened to the last maid I made friends with, but the grim looks the servants sent me after Sophia disappeared left me sick and hollow. That's one lesson I'll never need repeated.

I was too young to understand then. Distractions like friendships can't be tolerated. It's why I've spent my entire life in this villa, not even venturing as far as the nearest village. I must be the finest weapon ever forged if we're to succeed. The Godmothers need to be unforgiving because a mistake means our deaths. They can't be blamed if their methods appear severe to outsiders. *It's all Floren's fault.* If not for Floren, the Godmothers wouldn't be in this position.

A bird twitters outside.

"All right, all right. I'm finished. No need to scold me."

Ignoring the jar of salted fat on the pile of clothes, I dig through my chest of medicines until I find the blue jar with the balm I've perfected over the years. I smooth the salve on my cut, then cover it with a bandage. Much better—and my formula will ensure there won't be a scar.

A breeze from the open window stirs the stagnant air. I lift my face, inhaling deeply. *Chicken, lemon, ragu, pork, fresh bread.* My stomach gnaws on my backbone. The warm grain and milk served for breakfast was hours ago, and my supper isn't served until after sunset. *It would be irresponsible for me to faint in the middle of my lessons.*

In a flash, I'm dressed, the hem of the dress tucked up,

freeing my legs. A chair gives me easy access to the overhead window. There's nobody in the fields around the villa. *Perfect.* I cling to the outer wall, using well-worn finger- and toeholds to navigate to the roof.

When I reach the area over the kitchen window, I pause, listening to the servants gossip. I'd love to spend the day lying here in the sun and letting their voices drift over me, but someone will search for me soon.

My ears perk up at the clatter of a tray being set on the windowsill. In a flash, I'm down the wall and stuffing two cheese buns into my bodice, then back to the roof. A groan escapes me as I stuff half of the first warm bun in my mouth. The second half follows as I sprinkle some crumbs for the birds. I lick the grease off my fingers before climbing back down to the bathing chamber.

My mouth is full of cheesy goodness when the door flies open, banging against the wall.

Godmother Three barges in, wringing her hands. "She's here! She wants to see you!"

The muscles in my neck tighten, and I choke on the bread. I take off at a run. There's only one *she*—Godmother Twelve. The head of the Godmothers. *Something's happened. Something big.*

Godmothers gather in twos and threes, chattering excitedly as I race through the villa.

When did she get here? What happened, why is she back early? Is it time? I'm ready, I can do this.

I skid to a stop in front of an elaborately carved door. Smoothing my skirt, I take a deep breath, then knock.

There's a long pause, then a curt, "Come in."

Light plaster walls shimmer in the sunlight. Across from the windows sits a large map of the kingdoms covering most of the space, inviting the observer to study the details. My eyes go to the far end of the room. Godmother Twelve sits behind the large wooden desk, reading a stack of papers, a cup of tea to her right, the insignia of the Godmothers—a rose surrounded by a crown of thorns—conspicuous on the wall behind her. Her thick black hair is braided into a crown around her head, not a strand of silver marring the darkness, though she must be over sixty. Her beak nose prominent in her face, her dark amber eyes always watching, catching every detail.

Godmother Twelve is everything I wish I could be: elegant, intelligent, striking, and in control of every situation. My earliest memory is her wrapping my child's fist around a sword—barely bigger than a dagger—and telling me about my destiny to help the Godmothers. She's the one who encouraged me to learn about herbs, who brings me presents from her trips, since I can't leave the villa. Her duties take her away from our home often, but the other eleven Godmothers send her frequent updates on my progress.

I perch on the edge of the wooden chair in front of her desk. The cheese buns roll around my gut, and I curl my toes in my slippers. The buzz of insects outside the window is occasionally broken by the shuffle of papers. Only years of training keeps me from squirming in my seat.

Godmother Twelve taps the papers into a neat pile, then sets them aside. Her eyes narrow at the bandage on my neck.

I rub my hand across it, wincing at the unintended pressure on the cut.

She takes a long sip of tea, then looks at me over the rim. Her smile is as pleased as a cat full of cream. "The Floren king and queen have invited Princess Aryanna to visit as the first step in exploring a marriage alliance between the two kingdoms."

A drumming fills my chest and I lean forward, gripping the edge of my chair. If I was actually Princess Aryanna, I'd be horrified at the blatant attempt to show me off like a prized pig. Since I'm an imposter, I delight in Floren providing the method for their own demise. This is the perfect excuse for me to slip into the palace and get close to the royals without raising suspicions.

"I'll make those greedy, power-hungry men regret the day they removed the Godmothers from power. Floren was the first to revolt. It will be the first to pay." Her fists clench, then relax. "Godmother Eight will be your only instructor starting now. She'll also act as your Companion in Floren. We leave in a week." She picks the top sheet off the stack of papers and starts reading.

It's time! It's suddenly real in a way that it never was before. The room takes on a new importance, knowing this might be one of the last times I see it. I can't imagine calling another place home.

The Floren palace and royal family are a mystery. I know the basic facts, but realizing I'm going to soon put theory into practice shines a glaring light on the holes in my training. One slip and I'll be caught. If I can charm them, they're less likely to doubt me. *But how can I do that?* Knowing the queen is the third cousin of the Duke of Aemilia doesn't tell me if they prefer a joke or an interesting fact.

I clear my throat, trying to rid it of the scratchiness building there. "Godmother Twelve." I pause. *How can I put this without sounding unprepared?* "Could you tell me more about the royal family? Something about their personalities?"

Godmother Twelve eyes me sharply over her paper. "Why do you think I know them?"

"I—I don't." My mind races, wondering what put her off and how I can fix it. "But you're so thorough. You might have come across something in your research. I thought it would help me. When I'm in the palace. Make it easier to interact with them."

Her shoulders relax a fraction, and I breathe a silent sigh of relief.

"Royals don't think like that. You won't see them much."

"Surely they'll want the prince and princess to spend time together. Meals and meetings, and …" My voice trails off as Godmother Twelve shakes her head.

"Godmother Eight will manage the royals until we're ready to dethrone them. That's when we'll need your skills. Until then, stay away from the nobility at all costs."

With pleasure. I have bigger things to worry about than a spoiled prince and a bunch of boring nobles. I'm there to overthrow a kingdom.

They'll never see me coming.

This is it. I'll never go back to my old life, never see the villa again. If I succeed, the Godmothers will return to power, and we'll live happily ever after in Floren. If I fail … better not to be caught alive.

The carriage gives another jolt, my stomach matching the movement. The flapping curtains send flashes of light into the dark interior. Traveling across the country always sounded exciting, but I've spent most of my time trying to find a comfortable position on the carriage bench. I cross my ankles, then uncross them. Cross them again. Twist to the left, then twist to the right. Nothing seems to work. At least impersonating a princess means I have a great wardrobe. I smooth my hands over the soft fabric of my blue dress, admiring the shimmer of the fabric and how the color exactly matches my eyes. The white fur coat and thick boots complement the dress while keeping frostbite at bay. My breath makes small white puffs in the air as I tug the coat closed.

The past six days are a blur of carriage rides and dark

inns. Godmother Twelve has devoted the trip to reading from another endless pile of reports. Godmother Eight—Vivia, as I'm supposed to call her now—has spent every moment drilling me on everything from the Floren palace layout to the real Princess Aryanna's family to the Floren prince's favorite dessert.

But there's only so much facts and maps can do. Once I'm in the palace and among people, the real test begins. One slipup and my entire life's purpose goes up in flames. The Floren nobility should be easy enough to fool, but there's one person who could prove to be my biggest obstacle: Prince Nicolas.

I'll do my best to avoid him, but he might seek me out on his own. If the prince is against the marriage, he could make my life difficult and endanger my mission. I can't imagine he'll welcome me with open arms and poetry.

Prince Nicolas was pretty enough in his portrait, but the blank expression and stiff pose doesn't tell me much about his personality. *Is he adventurous? Surly? Kind? Would he rather go on a hunt or read in the library?* My curiosity means nothing. It's only natural I'd want to learn more about the people I'll be spending time with.

This morning, Godmother Eight—Vivia—focuses on watching the landscape instead of torturing me with questions. She stares out the window, occasionally tugging at the high collar of her dress or rubbing her throat. I try not to stare at the stark white stripe in her gray hair, but I find my gaze unwillingly drawn to it again and again as the hours pass in silence. When I was young, I overheard one of the servants saying the streak appeared because she's an evil fairy who goes around the kingdom cursing babies, and it grows wider with every new curse. Superstitious nonsense, of course. But the tale stuck with me, and I've been fascinated by her hair ever since.

There's a pang in my chest as I watch Godmother Twelve from under my lashes. Her copper dress is perfect, her face studious as she reads. All these days together, but we've barely spoken.

Godmother Twelve turns to Vivia. "We've received news. Certain prisoners disappearing from their cells. Supplies being diverted and smuggled out of the city." She raises her eyebrows at the other Godmother. "You'll need to look into it while you're at the palace."

More treachery by the Florens. "I can help search."

Godmother Twelve shakes her head. "This requires a subtle touch, and you'll attract too much attention. We have everything under control. Just focus on your role as the princess and leave this to us."

"But—"

Her face snaps into a severe frown. "You overstep yourself, Aryanna."

I flinch back. "I'm sorry."

"See that it doesn't happen again." She returns to the stacks of paper.

I swallow past the lump in my throat. *Foolish, foolish, foolish.* Godmother Twelve is only looking out for me. For all of us. She doesn't need me to make her job harder because I want to play the hero. My role is important; I don't need to take on more. Vivia will manage it.

Vivia says, "They're here." She dabs at the back of her neck with a handkerchief.

They turns out to be the entourage hired to escort us to Floren.

Apparently a princess requires an entire flock of servants

and guards. More people than we have at the villa. Twice as many. Four times. There must be at least fifty people milling around, tending to the picketed horses and the line of coaches and wagons lining the road. A large campfire is in the middle of the crowd, a huge iron kettle hanging over it. People stand chatting and eating from steaming bowls. About half are wearing guard uniforms, while the rest are a mix of work clothes and high-class servants. Hills gently roll away from the gathering, white frost decorating them.

Vivia climbs out, leaving us alone in the black carriage.

Godmother Twelve hands me a small wooden box with a smile. "I've brought you a luck present."

"Thank you!" I open it, finding three large brown stones inside. "What is it?"

"Apricot kernels." She plucks out a folded paper nestled on the side of the box.

I smooth out the sheet, my eyes feasting on the colorful fruit painted on the page along with a brief description of its uses, ranging from cyanide to cooking to helping the heart. I can't wait to add this to my collection. It's fascinating how something can have both healing and deadly components, nature balancing out the good and the bad.

She takes my hands in hers. "We've done all we can for you. Now it's your turn to serve. You will face unknown challenges, but you must succeed at all costs."

I nod solemnly, my cheeks flushed. "I understand."

"If you disobey Vivia or endanger the mission, I'll be very disappointed. Don't disappoint me." Her voice is iron.

I sit up straight. "I won't."

She kisses me on both cheeks, then steps out and walks to a waiting coach. She doesn't look back.

I close my eyes and lean my head back against the seat.

Once I leave the carriage, I'm no longer Aryanna, the girl who lives at the villa. I'll be Princess Aryanna of Cabriare. Everything depends on me.

My eyes flash open. *I'm ready.*

I push the door open and lift my skirt to descend.

"Princess, let me assist you." A boy in a guard's uniform rushes over.

He somehow manages to tangle the fabric around my legs, his jerky movements throwing me off balance. If not for all the fighting footwork I've done with Godmother Seven, I would've ended up face first in the slush. Not a great showing for my first princess performance. Safely on the ground, I shake out my skirt and pat my hair to verify my ebony waves are still in their elaborate braided hairstyle.

The boy beams, the gap between his front teeth in full view. "I've never met a princess before. It's an honor to escort you to Floren."

"The honor is mine." *I need to get rid of him before he breaks my neck helping me walk across the camp.* "Could you please convey my appreciation to the captain for escorting us? I know I'll be safe with you brave men guarding me."

He snaps a salute, his chest puffed out, then hurries off as Vivia joins me.

She crosses her arms, her tiny frame quivering with disapproval. "Are you trying to get caught? You are a *princess*. You don't ask, you command."

I keep the frown off my face as my stomach twists. *He didn't seem suspicious. Godmother Twelve surely won't hold this against me.*

Vivia doesn't wait for a response. She ushers me to the campfire, waving off anyone who tries to approach us. My boots squeak on the ice as we make our way to the benches set up at the fireside. She sips from a small flask smelling of honey, licorice, and mint.

Even though I'm only a curiosity, everyone's gazes keep me on edge. It's like someone's pointing an arrow at my back. I scoot closer to the fire, reaching my numb hands toward the flames, ordering myself sternly not to twitch. *Princesses don't fidget.*

Just as I thaw out, we're bundling into carriages and wagons. Mine is a lovely, small contraption with silver accents and an interior covered in a warm cream fabric. I sink into the comfortable seat, marveling at the softness. *Nobility really does live differently.*

Vivia sits on the bench across from me, pulling a thick blanket over her body. In moments, she's softly snoring.

A tall young man with a bashful smile opens the door and deposits warmed bricks at my feet before pressing a flagon into my hand, the smell of warmed wine and mulling spices tickling my nose. "Drink this, but small sips. It'll take the chill away." He ducks out of the doorway before I can thank him.

I sneak a peek at Vivia, then take a tiny mouthful. Rich sweetness floods my tongue, and a warmth travels to my stomach, spreading to my toes and fingers. *Wonderful.*

It seems like every five minutes, someone pops their head into the carriage to ask if I need anything or to offer a tidbit to snack on. My stomach soon bulges from packets of sugared nuts and warmed meat pies. The guards outside ride in a loose group, chatting and laughing among themselves, barely looking at the surrounding area. *A herd of horses wearing bells could sneak up on them. Good thing I can take care of myself. There's no telling what kind of highway robbers may lurk on the road.*

After a few hours, the carriage comes to a halt. The same gap-toothed young man who tripped me earlier opens the door and holds out a hand to assist me down. I glance at my sleeping companion and shrug. *No need to wake Vivia.*

Prepared this time, I manage the descent without incident. "We're stopping already?"

"Captain Necrini thought you'd like a brief rest, since long journeys can be difficult."

The quick stop involves building a fire to heat more wine and meat pies for the group. They gossip happily, some wandering into the woods to pick up firewood and explore, while others linger by the heat. I have to shake my head at their disorder. *It's a good thing Vivia is still asleep in the carriage, or she would have an apoplexy.*

As I turn away, my mind finally catches up with my eyes, and my mouth drops open.

The landscape has changed drastically in the scant few hours we've traveled. Gentle hills have transformed into snow-covered mountains. The forest crowds the road, the trees blanketed in fresh snowfall, creating a magical fairyland. A tangy scent fills the air, something I can't name, mixing with the wood smoke and warming pies. The wild beauty is so different from the cultivated farmland surrounding the villa.

My feet carry me closer to the trees as I admire the details on the bark and leaves. *They're so much prettier than their pictures.* I bounce on the balls of my feet, yearning to dive into the forest and explore, but my muscles lock into place. My bones ache at the memory of the beating Godmother One gave me the first and only time I tried to sneak out of the villa to see the village.

A trill echoes among the branches. A flash of yellow. *Is that a bird?* The play of light and shadow makes it hard to distinguish shapes. *A princess shouldn't go into the woods alone. She should stay with the group.*

A twig snaps. There's a splash of red among the foliage—not an animal.

Someone's watching me.

The red splash moves away, weaving through the trees parallel to the campsite. I crouch, stalking my prey from behind. A smile creeps over my face as I ease closer. *A proper test of my skills!* The snow-covered debris makes my movements louder than I wish, every squeak and crackle echoing in my ears, announcing my position.

My target is careful, but not careful enough. I close the gap. My muscles tense. A man. He's carrying a long sword, and two—no, three knives on his belt, plus one in his boot. The nondescript brown trousers and matching loose shirt might conceal more weapons. Dark hair, skin browned from the sun.

He reaches up and ties a piece of red fabric around the top half of his face.

A mask—he's definitely up to something. I scoop up a small branch as I continue my progress, heart pounding. What I wouldn't give for a sword or dagger right now. If I let the bandit get to the encampment, the guards will overcome him due to sheer numbers. Eventually. The bandit's movements and weapons confirm he's no stranger to combat. He'll catch the people at the campsite unawares. There could be casualties. Better to dispatch him here, quietly, away from the crowd. Nobody will be the wiser.

The man pauses, his hands busy with something at his chest. I come up behind him and brace my feet, aiming the branch at his unprotected head.

Quick as a fox, he spins, blocking the wood with twin daggers.

A trick!

The unexpected resistance throws me off balance, and I stagger back a half-step. The bandit is swift to press his advantage, knocking my arm to the side and swinging his knife toward my stomach. I automatically block his attack, using my other hand to bring the branch down on his undefended shoulder with a satisfying thump.

He grunts and jumps backward. I follow, feinting a strike at his arm and then aim for his thigh. He anticipates me, deflecting the blow, forcing me back to avoid his knife.

We circle each other, each breathing heavily. I eye his blades, longing to hold the steel in my hand and show this scoundrel what I can do when properly armed.

His teeth flash in a grin. "Are you lost, my lady? Perhaps you need assistance?"

I give him my sweetest smile. "I was going to ask you the same thing. Is that mask so you won't scare children with your hideous face?"

"It's because I don't want to blind you with my stunning good looks. One glance and you would be helpless."

"Then I'll leave it on when I bury your body. I wouldn't want a wandering wolf to fall in love with your corpse."

He holds a hand over his heart. "You wound me. How

could—"

He blocks my strike, blade flashing in the light. I drop my branch and twist his wrist, using the same maneuver Seven used on me, forcing him to release the knife. A kick to his knees and the bandit topples over. I scoop up the dagger and dart away, relishing the victory as he rolls to his feet.

I smirk as I face off against him, blade resting comfortably in my hand. "You seem to have dropped this."

"How kind of you to return it to me."

He lunges forward as I spring at him. I let my body move without thought, dodging and blocking his knife with mine. A part of me puzzles that he hasn't drawn his sword, but I shrug it off and plot how to get it away from him. He spins as I counter.

We're face to face, blades pressed against the other's throat, his arm wrapped around me and my hand pressing against his chest. His sea-gray eyes stare into my blue ones. I can count every freckle on the star-shaped pattern over his collarbone and smell the oranges he ate for lunch.

"It seems we're at an impasse. What a lovely inconvenience you are."

I pull my lips back in a feral grin. "I just find you inconvenient."

Laughter dances in those gray eyes. "That's twice you've injured me. A third time and I'll demand payment."

"If the dagger doesn't kill you, then I'm sure the blow to your ego will."

"Oh, ho, a challenge!"

Sensing his muscles tensing, I shove him away, twisting to escape his grip, slipping a second knife from his belt. He catches the back of the blasted skirt, pulling me down into the snow with him. I roll onto him, taking him by surprise, trapping his arms with my knees.

He breaks out in laughter. "Well played, Lady Lynx."

"You're awfully confident for someone with a dagger at his throat."

"I never hunt alone."

Cold steel presses against my neck.

Stupid, stupid, stupid. I quickly calculate my odds of taking them both on. Not good. I grudgingly raise my hands away from the bandit's throat.

A female voice says, "Drop the knives and get up."

The bandit winks. "Better do what she says. She doesn't have a sense of humor like me."

I angrily throw the knives side by side into a nearby tree, the hilts quivering with the impact. *Burn it, I had him!* I use both hands and a knee to shove off the bandit, forcing the air out of his lungs as I glare at him. It's tempting to kick him and wipe that amused expression off his face, but his rescuer would probably take it the wrong way. I cast one last venomous look at the scoundrel, then back away, turning to bring her into view.

She's shorter than me, but most girls are. Brown eyes, trousers, and a shirt that matches the bandit's dull-brown colors. It's hard to make out anything under the mask and enormous yellow hood she's wearing, but a strand of red hair has escaped its captivity. It's an amazing color, like embers in a fire. I'll recognize her by the hair alone if we ever cross paths again. *She better hope that day never comes.*

She gestures for me to back up. "We're leaving now. Count to fifty, then go back to your people. Don't follow us."

The bandit stands and brushes the snow off his clothes. "Mayhap she wants to come with us. What do you say, Lady Lynx?"

I fold my arms and tilt my head, pretending to consider it. "You'd better leave me behind. I'd have that dagger at your throat again soon enough, and your companion won't be around to save you."

She brandishes the sword. "I'd like to see you try."

He's right, she has no sense of humor.

The bandit gives me an elaborate bow. "My lady, it's been a pleasure. Perhaps one day we can pick up where we left off."

"I'll be happy to stab you anytime you wish."

His rich laugh rings through the trees as he walks a wide circle around me and retrieves the knives from the tree trunk. I tense, anticipating an attack, but the only sound is retreating footsteps. Wasting no time, I duck to the side and run for cover in case they come back. The forest looks empty, no sign of the two outlaws except their vanishing footprints.

I huff in disgust. *Lady Lynx! That overblown ego needs puncturing!* I grudgingly admit he's a skilled fighter. *My first bout outside the villa, and I've failed.* Godmother Seven's voice chimes in, saying my performance was shameful. My lips tug into a smile. But it was exciting. Fun. If we meet again, it might be worth sparing his life so I can keep fighting with him.

Odd they didn't kill me or try to take me hostage when they had the chance. Certainly, they had every opportunity to.

I hurry back to the campfire, but my haste is unnecessary. The group is wandering around the area, still gossiping and eating. Nobody appears to have noted my absence.

A woman in a long buttercream dress spots me. "Princess, heavens! Your hair is half out of its pins! And your dress! That must have been a vigorous walk."

She leads me to the fireside, then moves behind me and plucks the pins from my hair. As the last waves fall loose, she gently finger-combs the strands out. Another woman drops a blanket over my shoulders.

The young man from earlier hurries over and hands me a warmed meat pie, then places a flask on the ground. "I'll warm more bricks for the next part of the trip."

Playing a princess definitely has more advantages than I expected. But I can't relax and enjoy it. I keep my eyes on the woods, watching for color between the trees.

Vivia will have a fit when she finds out what I did. It was foolish. The heavens only know what kind of punishment she'll devise for putting myself and our mission in danger. Fighting with the bandit was an unnecessary risk and a useless waste of time. He's arrogant and annoying. It's best to forget about him.

I close my eyes and press my fingers to my lips. *I hope I get to cross swords with him again soon.*

5

Floren is a shock to the senses. The facts and statistics from the Godmothers crumble in the face of reality. It's impossible to take in all the incredible and marvelous things as we wind through the city streets. I could never imagine so many people in one place, and that's only what I can see out the carriage window. People in every shape and size and color, from pale as a sunbeam to dark as the night sky, and everything in between. The bright colors mingle with the deafening noise of the people, horses, and merchants hawking their wares. Scents change with every turn of the carriage wheel, from roasting meats to spices to sewers to perfumes.

And the palace! An imposing white building sitting atop the hill, the city spread out at its feet. Cavernous rooms with gilding and paintings on every surface, vases of flowers, and soft couches and chairs begging for occupants. Crystal chandeliers floating impossibly high overhead, tapestries breathing life into the fantastical animals and scenery. Each room a new story, a new adventure. I could spend days in the marbled welcome hall alone, examining all the wonders.

Even my suite of rooms is overly lavish. My room at the villa was a fraction of the size of the closet. There's no reason a person should have a sitting room, bathing chamber, study, and bedroom to themselves. At least they're a pleasing pale-green color instead of the garish color scheme adorning the rest of the palace.

Vivia's stuck to my side since she saw my damp and dirty dress. Luckily, we haven't had a moment alone together. Between my entourage constantly checking on me, the Floren escort that joined us at their border, and the palace-assigned servants and helpers, I've been surrounded. Never have I been so grateful for so little privacy.

An attendant bustles Vivia out of the room to oversee unpacking the luggage, while another guides me to the bathing chamber, her movements revealing a slight limp. Her white hair hangs in a long braid down her back, a stark contrast to the pinned hair in fashion with the other women.

The short woman tsks as she tests the water. "Too cool. I'll have them bring up another kettle."

I trace the ivy pattern on the wall, admiring the painter's skill. "I'm sure it's warm enough." The chamber is a work of art, a beautiful green marble on three of the four walls, ceiling, and floor. The fourth has a painted plaster woodland scene with small creatures peeking between the ivy and bushes. In the middle of the chamber is the huge sunken bathtub, big enough to swim laps in.

"Oh no, Your Highness." She looks around, then lowers her voice. "The king and queen insist on nothing but the best for you. They want you to feel welcome."

Her air of imparting a great secret to me is touching, although I fail to see the importance she places on the information. "Really, it's fine. I'm eager to wash the road dust away." My skin itches looking at the clean water filled with bubbles and smelling of lavender.

She helps unlace the dress, and I pull it off, laying it on a nearby chair. I pause, waiting for her to go. She looks at me expectantly.

Blushing furiously, I turn away and strip off my smallclothes, then dive into the water. When I bathed at the villa, servants were always popping in and out. I don't know why it's different having someone watching me here, but it is.

The woman hums as she picks up my discarded clothes and lays out a fresh towel before leaving.

Now she goes! At least I don't have to run to the closet naked. I quickly scrub off the road grit and dust, dunking my hair and lathering soap into the waist-length tresses. I'm rinsing the last of the suds out when yet another attendant enters.

She rolls up her sleeves. "Please, my lady, allow me." She wipes her hands on her brown dress, then takes a bottle off a shelf and gestures me to the side of the tub.

I paddle over, wary of what she has in mind. When she turns me so my back faces her, I tense, ready for an attack. Instead, she pours something that smells fresh and citrusy over my head and massages it into my scalp. My eyes slide closed, and my muscles turn to pudding. All the tension drains out of me. My mind drifts into a pleasant haze as she continues her ministrations.

When she stops, I bite my lip, on the verge of begging her to keep going. She uses a jug from the shelf to rinse my hair, then gently rubs it with a towel.

"Thank you," I sigh, fully relaxed from the bath and her

gentle touch.

Her hands pause for a moment. "My pleasure."

The first woman bustles back and holds up the towel. "They're ready for you, Princess."

The attendants in the room have multiplied like field mice since I left. They stuff me into a heavy green dress that makes it impossible to breathe. I spend the next two hours being brushed, painted, buffed, and decorated within an inch of my life. A fistfight almost breaks out among the ladies deciding what perfume I should wear, although why I need additional scents after the bath is beyond me. I can't tell if these are Floren attendants or from my own hired entourage. There's no way to ask, lest I give away I'm an imposter. Mostly I try to sit quietly and smile at my helpers as they treat me like a living doll.

From their chatter, I gather I'll be presented to the court shortly and meet the royal family. Godmother Twelve was very specific in how I should act when I meet Prince Nicolas: unassuming, shy, sweet. Do nothing that arouses suspicion or calls attention to myself. Basically, I should be as interesting as a doorstop, but less useful.

My toes curl in my slippers. *Where is Vivia? How long can it take to unpack a few dresses?* My impatience increases as each minute ticks off on the timepiece sitting on the desk. We rehearsed the simple ceremony numerous times, so I can do it in my sleep, but I didn't expect to face the court alone on my first day. Godmother Twelve wants Vivia to manage the royals, not me.

The white-haired attendant with the limp watches from the side of the room, her eyes brimming with tears. "You look so lovely. The prince will fall in love with you the moment he sees you."

That would make things easier. A lovesick prince would be less trouble than an irritated one. *What would a clay-brained princess say?* "Do you really think so? Do you think he's kind?"

"The servants here have nothing but kind words about him. I think you'll be very happy once you get to know him."

They are *from my entourage. I'm glad I didn't say anything.* Somehow, I'll have to find out their names without letting on my ignorance. *Would the Cabriaren princess know their names?* The Godmothers are making this more difficult than it needs to be. Why not properly introduce me to everyone, so I recognize who is on our side? Godmother Twelve must have more spies in the ranks than me and Vivia, but I don't know how to find them.

Yet another maid bustles in with a bowl of fresh flowers, followed by another holding a veil.

"It's time."

The announcement sends the attendants into a tizzy. They flutter around me, smoothing out invisible wrinkles and pinning the flowers and veil to the simple tiara on my head. The lace is thick, effectively cutting off my vision, making everything around me appear as fuzzy shapes. *Probably done on purpose to keep the real princess from running away.*

The attendants take my arms and guide me out of the room. I focus on not tripping over my feet as they lead me blindly through the hallways. *Burning veil. Might as well have blindfolded me.* By counting the steps and turns against the map I memorized, they appear to be leading me to the receiving hall. There's barely a pause in a small side room, then they're shoving me out the door as the music swells.

I walk slowly forward, hands clasped in front of me like a good little princess, keeping my head level and my steps even. My mind buzzes with an exhausted energy from sleepless nights and excitement. The small blobs ahead are probably the royal family, but for all I know they could be giant bags stuffed full of weasels. *Why did they make this burning thing so thick?* Slowly it dawns on me the rapid breathing ringing in my ears is coming from me. I clamp my lips shut. *On the bright side, if I can't see them, they can't see me.* I drop the vague smile and let my face relax. When the blobs turn finally into large blobs, I drop into a deep curtsy.

The majordomo intones, "Your Majesties, Princess Aryanna Erica Coltello of Cabriare, presenting herself to Prince Nicolas Antonio Lukas Scoletti of Floren."

Finally, I can get out of this suffocating thing. I paste what I hope is a shy and hopeful smile on my face as the prince lifts the veil.

A grin spreads across his face, and his gray eyes twinkle. He whispers just loud enough for me to hear, "Hello, Lady Lynx."

6

My stomach drops.

People keep talking, but I can't hear them over the roaring in my ears. *The prince will never believe the shy, demure princess I'm supposed to play. Why, oh why, did I hunt him down in the forest? If I had stayed with the group instead of going off on a lark, things would still be going according to plan. And why was he there? A prince shouldn't wander around the woods in disguise. It's really his fault for putting me in this situation. Everything the Godmothers have planned is in jeopardy. I cannot fail. I will not fail. This can still work. I can turn this to my advantage.*

Thunderous applause breaks me out of my mental whirlwind. I take Nicolas's arm and we walk to the banquet hall across the wing, his chuckles ringing in my ears. My shoulders tighten, and I clench my jaw. I do my best to ignore his gleeful teasing as we stand in the receiving line to greet each guest.

He smirks. "You seem a bit pale. May I have someone fetch you a glass of wine?"

Only if I can dump it over your head. I bite the inside of my cheek, sending a smile that promises he'll pay for this later. "That's so kind of you, but I'm fine. Would you care for one?"

"Mayhap later."

He squeezes my hand. I grip it back, trying to crush his fingers.

The receiving line goes on for hours. It seems every person in the kingdom wants to exchange words with the heir to the throne and drop thinly veiled hints about their hope for a marriage announcement. It's a funny mix of people: the expected nobility, of course, but also people in plainer clothes with rough hands. *Floren's customs are stranger than I thought.*

At long last, the receiving line ends, and the banquet begins. It's an impressive display. A gallery hidden in the second floor holds musicians sending sweet music over the diners. Jewels and silks dazzle in the candlelight. The tables are set with golden plates and glasses that sparkle against the dark-red tablecloths. Delicious smells of roasting meats and steamed fish fill the air.

Protocol places me between the prince and a noble who is deaf, judging by the way he keeps turning his head and throwing out random responses when nobody is speaking to him.

Prince Nicolas leans toward me. "Well, my little lynx. I didn't expect to run into you so soon. This is a most pleasant turn of events."

"I'm glad one of us is enjoying this."

I give myself a mental smack. I need to lull him into relaxing around me, not spar with him. Obviously, the innocent princess persona won't work, but that doesn't mean

I can't be sweet to him now. He'll forget all about the minor incident in the woods and let his guard down. *Yes, yes, good plan.*

"Your Highness—"

"So formal, Lady Lynx! Someone who's held a knife to my throat should call me Nicolas."

I grit my teeth. "Nicolas. Please, call me Aryanna." *For the love of my sanity, please, please call me Aryanna.* "We started off badly. I didn't mean—"

"To attack your future betrothed? I imagine not." He chuckles and takes my hand. "You can make it up to me by telling me how handsome you find me. And humble. I know you think I'm humble."

I snatch my hand away. "Only if I was blind and deaf," I mutter. *The man is infuriating! Not even Seven can make me lose my temper this fast.* "It was all a simple misunderstanding. I wasn't going to hurt you."

"My pride would disagree, darling." Nicolas raises his wineglass. "A toast to you. A woman who will keep a man honest with her wit. And when that doesn't work, she'll stab him."

He takes a big swig as I narrow my eyes and hold my fork in a death grip. *There's a lot of ways utensils can inflict pain.* I'd better move the conversation to something safe. "I've been told you have an excellent hedge maze."

"Hmm? Oh, yes. It's a bit tame for someone like you. Meant for ladies. You need something more suitable for your … passionate nature."

I put my hands flat on the table to keep from wrapping them around his neck. "What would you suggest?"

Nicolas's grin turns mischievous. "I'm sure I can come up with something."

After the interminable banquet, Nicolas escorts me cut of the dining hall to where an attendant is waiting to guide me back to my suite. Unnecessary since I've memorized the palace layout, but I need to keep up my appearance as the ignorant foreign princess.

Nicolas presses a kiss to the back of my hand. "Allow me to escort you to your rooms."

My guide stifles a gasp.

The prince's impropriety will be all over the kingdom by morning! He might not care for his reputation, but I have to have a care for mine. *If Vivia reports to Godmother Twelve I'm playing the floozy to the prince—wait, this can work to my advantage. Rumors of a lovesick prince are better than a suspicious one. If the Godmothers believe the prince is smitten with me, they'll think I'm following the plan*

I lower my lashes and murmur a demurral.

"Why so shy, Lady Lynx? You weren't this quiet during our last—" His eyes dart to the woman hanging on every word. "—meeting."

"I'm glad I made such an impression on you, since I don't recall much about it." I raise an eyebrow at him, letting my lips twitch.

"Oh, you definitely made an impression. Mostly on my ribs." He rubs his side. "I'll be happy to refresh your memory tomorrow. Good night." He bows over my hand, then whistles as he strides down the hallway.

Insufferable! I look forward to the day I can properly teach him a lesson with my sword. But for now, I'll limit myself to trading verbal barbs. Better than making dull conversation about the weather or fashion or whatever nobles care about. And it seems to entertain him. *If I can keep his interest while having a bit of fun myself, then all the better.* I replay our exchange during supper as my lips curve into a smile. *Nobody's ever teased me before.*

The attendant is watching me with wide eyes.

"Shall we?"

She starts, then leads me through the maze of the palace. I match the path with the map in my head, noting key rooms to investigate and any details that seem out of place. It's hard to see past the chaotic color and trinkets, but a few spots look worthy of visiting later.

The woman stops in front of the two large doors to my suite. "Do you need anything else, Princess?"

"No, thank you. Good evening."

Her face breaks out in a smile and she curtsies. "Good evening, my lady." She scurries down the hall, eager I'm sure to share the scandalous scene between the prince and me with the other staff.

Still, I can't be too mad. I enjoyed every exchange as much as he did. It's so freeing not to worry about watching every word, to have an audience who appreciates my remarks instead of punishing me. To just react instead of controlling every action and thought. Seeing his gray eyes light up when I delivered a clever taunt was so rewarding. Oh yes, interacting with Nicolas can be quite intoxicating. I'll have to watch myself and make sure I don't overindulge.

Lost in thought, I push open the doors to my room. The white-haired woman with the limp jumps up from the chair in the sitting room.

"Princess, Lady Vivia has fallen ill."

Vivia? Oh, Godmother Eight. That explains her absence. "Where is she? Please, take me to her." *There must be something in my medicine collection that can help.*

The wrinkles at the corners of her eyes deepen. "I'm so sorry, I can't. The doctors worry it may be contagious. They've ordered no visitors, but I can get a message to her if you wish."

I freeze, keeping my expression neutral. *No visitors? But Godmother Eight is supposed to instruct me, tell me when it's time for the takeover. I don't have a way to contact Godmother Twelve.* My hands leave a clammy streak on my skirt. *What if it's going to happen tomorrow? Or the next day? Surely the Godmothers don't expect me to linger in the palace too long.*

We have to wait for the perfect moment, but every day is another risk of discovery. Knowing Godmother Twelve, there's probably three plans in place with at least five contingency plans. It will take a coordinated effort to get the royal family away from their guards and smuggle them out of the palace undetected. It's crucial I'm ready when the Godmothers need me. If one of the royals gets away, they'll be a threat to the Godmothers' rule. It's going to be near impossible to figure out what Godmother Twelve wants me to do without Vivia here.

But nearly impossible isn't impossible. I won't sit around sipping tea and doing nothing.

If Godmother Eight isn't around to help me, I'll do it myself. There's no need to have someone shadowing my every move; I've been training for this my entire life. *I'll learn everything about the royals and the goings on at the palace. I'll be ready to act when the Godmothers need me.*

The woman is still waiting for me to respond.

What would the princess say? "Please pass along my concern for Lady Vivia's health, and tell her ..." *When will I know the burning rebellion is underway?* "I'll miss her wisdom." *There, safe enough.*

The attendant beams. "Wonderful. Until she's regained her health, I'll be assisting you. My name is Gaia."

"Thank you, Gaia. Please, call me Aryanna." My mind goes back to the chest of medicines in my luggage. "What's befallen her?"

She shakes her head. "The servants couldn't tell me more than that she collapsed. But the doctors here are very knowledgeable. I'm sure she's in good hands."

I want to press further, but I can't risk arousing her suspicions. "I'm sure you're right. My apologies, today's been overwhelming. I just want to go to bed." I rub my head for effect.

She helps me undress and hangs the clothes somewhere in the closet's depths. There's a fresh nightshift lying on the dresser that I slip over my head, then wash my face and brush my teeth with the tooth powder laying by the basin. I slide into bed, luxuriating in the silk sheets and warm blankets. Someone was kind enough to put a bed warmer between the layers to chase away the chill.

Gaia pulls up the blankets and blows out the candles, then pats the coverlet. "Good night, sweetling."

After she leaves, I stare at the canopy overhead, mulling over the day's events. My first day as nobility, I get into a knife fight with the prince I'm supposed to avoid, destroying my cover as a shy, unassuming princess. My superior falls ill, leaving me cut off from the Godmothers and without direction. Now a stranger is assigned to watch my every move. Probably the most disastrous first day of royalty in history.

I'm afraid to see what tomorrow will bring, especially after the prince's worrying promise to entertain me. The heavens only know what he's planning.

I wiggle down in the sheets and grin at the ceiling. *I can't wait to find out.*

8

Gaia throws the curtains open. "Good morning, sweetling. You have a big day ahead of you."

I rub the sleep from my eyes. "Is something happening?" My mind's still in a wonderful haze. I can't remember ever sleeping that well. The layers of blankets wrap me in a lovely cocoon of warmth, keeping the faint chill at bay.

She tugs open another set of curtains. "The king and queen have invited you to breakfast. They heard about your ill companion and wanted to make sure you're doing well in her absence."

"Th—that's nice of them." *Too nice.* Why are they concerned about a sick servant? Vivia means nothing to them. Unless they suspect something.

"They're wonderful people. I'll get your dress ready while you bathe. The tub's ready."

Did a whole troupe of people parade through here while I slept? Filling that enormous tub must take hours. I don't want strangers wandering in and out of my rooms. "That isn't necessary. I can make do with a hip bath. Please don't go to the trouble tomorrow."

She gives me an odd look, then her sunny smile returns. "It's no problem at all, sweetling. Let us spoil you. This must be overwhelming, coming to a strange place and losing your companion all in one day. A little pampering will do you some good."

Since I can't find a way to argue with that, it's best to surrender gracefully. "Thank you. And please, thank everyone who helped." She's one to keep an eye on. There must be an ulterior motive behind that cheery act.

The tub is just as wonderful today as it was yesterday. I take my time, enjoying the heat soaking into my muscles. I could spend all day in here, but I reluctantly force myself to get out before the water cools. The royal family shouldn't be kept waiting. A worm of guilt works its way through my head, but I shake it off. *One breakfast with the royals won't harm anything. If Vivia's not here, I need to learn their actions and evaluate their defenses, and this is the best way to start.*

Gaia's selected a rose-red dress with matching beadwork on the neckline and sleeves. Some might find it plain, but it's beautiful for the simplicity. She puts my ebony waves into a simple twist and then hands me off to an attendant waiting outside the doors to escort me. He takes a different path to the royal dining room than I would have. I make note of the changes to study later to determine if the alternative route has any advantages I'd not considered.

Despite my long soak, I've arrived before anyone else. It's a light, airy room compared to the rest of the palace. A pale yellow on the walls with no other decorations or paintings. A long line of windows across the entrance lets the sunlight pour in through thin lace curtains. Servants are positioned around the room and next to the long buffet. The dark walnut dining table is surprisingly small, with room for six people at the most.

I start toward the buffet, but one servant clears his throat and holds out a chair. Heat fills my cheeks as I slide into the seat. It's so hard to remember to act like a princess when my first instinct is to do things for myself.

Nicolas strides into the room and slaps my helper on the back. "Tonio, my good man. How is Elena?"

"Getting bigger every day. I swear I can see her grow as she stands in front of me."

"Make sure Rosa gives you a slice of that lemon honey cake to take home to her."

"Thank you, sire. You know what a sweet tooth she has."

Nicolas takes the chair across from me. "Good morning. I'm sorry your companion's ill."

I search his face but find only sincerity. "I'd like to see her."

"The doctors say it's too dangerous for anyone else to be around her." He gives me a sympathetic look. "You'll be the first visitor as soon as they lift the restrictions. Until then, I'll make sure they send you daily updates."

Does the prince have a twin brother they didn't tell me about? Who is this considerate stranger?

I'm saved from replying by the king and queen arriving. It's the first chance I have to study them since I was distracted at the introduction ceremony and banquet. The king's beard is liberally sprinkled with silver, while the queen's dark hair shines without a hint of white. Something about her tranquil smile and confidence makes me believe she'll be comfortable with her appearance at any age. Their names drift to the surface: Luka and Renata.

I jump up and curtsy, but the queen waves me off.

"Please, sit. We're very informal when it's just family."

The king kisses me on both cheeks, his beard tickling my skin. "Welcome to Floren. We're so happy to have you with us."

The queen takes my hands. "We're terribly sorry about your companion. I feel awful that your parents couldn't accompany you, and now she's ill too. Please rest assured we have our most talented people taking care of her. If you need anything, just ask." She studies my face, then shakes her head. "Forgive my staring, dear. You look so much like your mother."

I murmur my thanks and resist the urge to fidget. *These are the coldhearted tyrants the Godmothers told me about? They're excellent actors. Highly convincing. I can see why they've fooled so many people over the years.*

The queen kisses me on the cheek, then takes the seat next to mine while the king sits next to Nicolas, leaving the chairs at the head and foot of the table empty. The servers spring into action, presenting dishes from the sideboard and doling out portions.

My mouth waters at the selection. I was too preoccupied to eat supper, and the snacks from the carriage ride were far too long ago. It's tempting to grab the bowl of eggs from Tonio and dump the whole thing onto my plate. It hurts to turn down most of the options and only select a few items to keep up the dainty princess act. I promise my complaining stomach I'll dig out one of the smuggled packets of glazed nuts from yesterday as soon as I get back to my rooms.

Nobody else seems concerned with appearances. They load up their plates with hearty piles, eating eagerly.

The queen casts a concerned look at my scant selection. "Is there anything else we can get you, Aryanna? Our cook would be happy to make you something."

"Thank you, Your Majesty. I'm fine." I scoop up a bit of hot grain drizzled with treacle while my stomach begs for more. The packet of nuts shrinks smaller and smaller in my mind.

"Call me Renata." She gestures to a server. "Please, try this. It's Rosa's specialty. She's quite proud of it and would never forgive me if I didn't persuade you to taste it."

The woman puts a small plate in front of me holding two long buns sliced in half and stuffed with cream. I press my lips together to keep from drooling at the warm sugar smells floating up from the treat.

It would be rude to reject a gift from the queen. I snatch up a bun and inhale deeply, then sink my teeth into the treat. "Oooooh." I can't stop the moan that escapes as the flavor explodes on my tongue. The cream blends perfectly with the bun, with just the tiniest hint of lemon tartness to keep the sweetness from being overwhelming. I take another bite, savoring the pastry. *I could die happy right now.*

"Maritozzi!" Nicolas grabs the other treat off the plate and takes a huge bite.

The queen frowns at him, her lips twitching. "Nicolas, that's for our guest." The disapproving expression dissolves into laughter as the prince gives his mother an innocent look and bats his eyes. "You're incorrigible."

The king gives a hearty laugh. "He gets it from you." He steals the bun from his son and takes a bite. "Delicious."

Nicolas eyes my pastry. I pull it safely out of his reach.

She shakes her head and looks at me. "Forgive their deplorable lack of manners. I can barely get them to behave in public. During our private times it's mayhem."

The king points the bun at her. "We all deserve time to be lunatics. Between the nobles and the Council, it's astonishing we can accomplish anything. Look how long it took to get them to agree to fix the sewers in the lower wards."

The queen's hand flies to her mouth. "Luka! We don't discuss sewers during meals. What will our guest think?"

Nicolas shrugs, then filches the last bite of pastry from his father. "Aryanna doesn't mind. Anyone who can wield a dagger with skill isn't going to be put off by sewers. She fits right in."

I bite my cheek to stop the smile threatening to break out. *No need to get fluttery over a few words. Besides, I'm sure he meant that as an insult.*

The queen raises an eyebrow. "And how would you know? Were you having a knife fight at supper that I missed?"

When the prince squirms, I can't resist chiming in. "Yes, I'm sure your mother would be interested in hearing *all* about how we met."

The king frowns. "You didn't meet at the ceremony? How is this possible?"

The discomfort in Nicolas's eyes surprises me. Once I found out his identity, I figured his visit in the woods was an innocent prank on the visiting princess. Was he up to something malicious? Something that ties to the horror stories the Godmothers told me? His obvious unhappiness means there's more than meets the eye. His parents will pry the truth out of him.

The prince turns to me with a pleading look.

Burn it. "It's really my fault. I sent him a note and asked him to meet me outside the city. I—I'm sorry, I shouldn't have. It's ridiculous, but I didn't want the first time we met to be in front of a crowd." I lower my eyes, letting my hair fall forward so I can smirk at him without his parents seeing. "I can be a bit timid."

Nicolas leans back in his chair, covering his chuckle with a cough.

The king's shoulders relax. "Ah, is that all? Understandable, my dear. Why, when I met Renata, my knees were shaking so badly, I fell flat on my face. Not the best impression. Thank the heavens she looked past that."

"That's when I knew we would be happy, my love." She puts her hand across the table.

The king covers her hand with his, gazing at her with adoring eyes.

I look away from the intimate moment, swallowing around the lump in my throat. I wonder if my parents were as in love as the king and queen are. The Godmothers never told me much about them, only that they died fighting for the Godmothers, and they wanted me to take up the war in their place. When I was little, I would imagine how my parents looked and what they were like. The phantom parents I created were a lot like King Luka and Queen Renata: loving, funny, attractive, and filled with happiness.

Nicolas is watching me, his head tilted, a curious expression on his face. I brush the corners of my eyes and stand, cutting off the conversation at the table.

"Excuse me. I—I'm not feeling very well." I turn and flee.

I storm into my rooms and throw myself down on the couch, wrapping my arms around a pillow. *How could I get so emotional over nothing? Don't I have any control over myself?* I can't let that happen again.

It's only been a day, and everything is turned on its head. Life was so simple when I was at the villa. I knew who the enemy was and what I had to do. Here everything's confused. I thought I was prepared to play Princess Aryanna, but I had no idea how hard it would be.

And that's all I am: a pale imitation of the real princess. I'm her ghost. Based on her portrait, we look similar enough to be sisters, but not twins. My eyes are two shades bluer, and her nose tips up at the end while mine is straight. Close enough to pass scrutiny for people who have heard of the princess, or seen her from afar, which the Godmothers assure me will be adequate. Nobody at the court has met Princess Aryanna in person except the Floren envoy to Cabriare, and they'll be absent during my stay.

Even so, I can't cut my hair because her hair is long. I

can't spend time in the sun because she doesn't have freckles. I can't bite my nails, or get a scrape, or chip a tooth. But what happens to her happens to me. I know she has a scar on her left foot because the Godmothers cut me in the same place. She plays the harp, so I play the harp. They've spent every moment of my life shaping me into her. My name isn't even my own—it's *hers*.

That doesn't leave any room for me. What I want. *Who am I?* I can't answer that question.

No—I'm a weapon for the Godmothers. The princess can't say that. She's an ornament, a pawn. I am steel. I'll be the blade that cuts the rot out of this kingdom. Those who abuse their power must be stopped by those with the strength to fight.

But I need to know who that is.

While I'm part of the Godmothers' plans, I haven't learned the whole of them. They guard their secrets carefully, which is why they've survived this long. If the Godmothers say the king and queen are guilty, then they are. I'll find the proof and root out their coconspirators. That will make it easier to determine who to remove when it's time to act, and who might be swayed to our side.

From now on, I'll avoid the royals as much as I can and guard my emotions around them when I can't. Be polite and pleasant, but that's all. Learn everything I need about them to ensure the Godmothers succeed.

Once the twelve Godmothers are restored to their rightful place, I'll have a normal life. Friends and hobbies that don't involve impersonating a foreign princess. That day I can leave "Princess Aryanna" behind and find out who I really am.

A name of my own instead of *hers*. To have someone

see *me* and not her.

Gaia hums as she comes into the room. "You're back early." She peers closer. "Are you feeling well, sweetling?"

"I'm fine, just a bit of a headache." I sit up and smooth back my hair, using the motion to wipe the tears away. "How is Lady Vivia?"

"The doctors still aren't sure what's ailing her, but her condition hasn't worsened."

"I wish I could help her." There's so many herbs and concoctions Godmother Twelve has given me over the years; surely one of them would be beneficial. *She was dabbing her head and rubbing her throat on the way here, so likely a fever and sore throat.* I have willow bark, honey, licorice, coriander, mint …

"I know it's frustrating, but it's too risky. The king and queen worry you'll fall ill."

Or they wanted a reason to separate me from Vivia. Isolate me so I'm weak. Little do they know I'm just as dangerous on my own.

Gaia sails into the bedroom and returns in a moment with a lilac dress with gold insets in the skirt. She checks the timepiece on the table as she drapes the dress over the chair. "If you'd like, you can take a quick nap before the party."

All thoughts of Vivia fly out of my head. "What party?"

"Lady Rosamund is hosting an ice party for you in the gardens. It's one of the traditional Floren celebrations this time of year. The queen will be in attendance, along with most of the court ladies."

My heart sinks. *Of course, the princess has events she's expected to attend.* Vivia surely had a plan to get me out of them, but the only idea I come up with is to fake an illness, and that will get me quarantined. *Better to stay free and play along.* "What other activities do I have scheduled?"

Gaia launches into a list of luncheons, teas, plays, performances, balls, and outings. Every moment of my day for the next week is planned from waking to well past sunset. Each activity adds a stone to my gut. It's unlikely I'll find conspiracies at a garden party or be able to discuss the ways the king and queen oppress citizens over tea. Not to mention being on display every hour of every day sounds exhausting. "Don't I have any free time?"

She looks uncomfortable. "Their majesties wanted to make you feel welcome. They're introducing you to their people and letting them get to know you. They want you to think of Floren as your home."

The real Aryanna's home. No—this is my home now, not hers. After the Godmothers take over, I'll stay here in the palace with them. I view my suite with pursed lips. It's still ridiculously large, but I'll get used to it. I can add a few touches, something that's mine and mine alone, to make it feel like I belong here. *Yes, this can work.*

And Gaia is right. This is a chance to get to know the people here and find out who is trustworthy and who is loyal to the royals. A garden party is as good a place to start as any to search for the king and queen's accomplices.

So much for keeping my distance from the nobility. "Lady Rosamund is on the Floren Council, correct?"

If I can't beat them, join them.

Then crush them at their own game.

Gaia bundles me to within an inch of my life, all the

time tutting over the cold and fear of my catching a chill. Three layers of smallclothes under the thick wool purple dress make it hard to walk, while the long fur coat, gloves, and fur hat threaten to smother me. Then she has the gall to abandon me at the entrance to the garden, insisting it wouldn't be proper for her to attend despite her role as my acting companion.

At least the setting is pleasant. Fantastical ice sculptures decorate the garden, while hidden musicians fill the air, making it appear that I've stepped into a fairy ice land. Between the frost-covered hedges and decorations are benches for the ladies to perch on. Cauldrons of hot cider and spiced wine steam in the cool winter air. Servers carry trays with fig cookies, almond macaroons, panforte, and other delights to tempt the appetite. Even so, only the Florens are strange enough to believe an outdoor party is fun when there's snow on the ground.

Calling my attempts at chitchat pathetic would be kind. *Appalling* is a better description. The two Council members in attendance, Lady Rosamund and Lady Elisabetta, give me pitying looks as I stumble through the history of the Floren currency. Lady Maria, who has ties to Linaria—a country that's always worth keeping an eye on—gets visibly upset and storms off when I can't tell her if hats are in fashion in Cabriare. The Godmothers should have spent more time on idle gossip skills and less time making me memorize trade routes.

I give up after the third noblewoman pats me on the shoulder with an understanding smile and switches the conversation to the weather. Letting the women prattle on about their own interests seems to make them happy and stops the sympathetic gazes.

Talking to Gaia or even Nicolas is so much easier than dealing with the ladies at the party. I can't pinpoint the difference, but conversations flow naturally with them. Every interaction here leaves me exhausted.

I finally escape a noblewoman intent on describing every blade of grass on her sheep farm and slowly totter through the gardens until the noise fades. A sunken garden provides the perfect cover to take a moment and catch my breath, the high hedges around the perimeter hiding me from any prying eyes. Before I can sit on the little bench set in front of the frozen fountain, shrill voices approach. I duck inside a wide hedge, holding my breath as three of the more annoying ladies from the party appear.

"The princess came this way, I'm sure." The first woman peers through her spectacles, the bells on her small hat tinkling with the movement.

The youngest one chirps, "Mayhap she went to the farther pond." She tugs on one of her long ringlets.

The third woman wrinkles her nose in her pinched face. "Or got lost in the maze. A bit dimwitted, isn't she?" She pats the tower of poorly dyed blond hair piled on her head, arranged around a golden cage.

I grind my teeth as they titter. The lot of them are cackling hens. They weren't so quick to insult me when they were simpering and offering me invitations.

"Who are we hiding from?" Nicolas whispers.

I squeak, then slap my hands over my mouth. The women chatter steps away from us, seemingly undisturbed by our noise.

The prince presses a finger to his lips as he silently laughs. I glare and elbow him in the ribs. He presses closer, peering around me to the sunken garden. Impossibly, the heat from his body makes its way through my thick layers of clothes, warming my back. My breath catches. I try to squirm away, but there's no space to move without exposing my hiding spot.

To my horror, the bespectacled woman sits on the bench, tugging her woolen wrap tighter around her shoulders. "You don't really believe the prince is interested in that foreigner, do you?"

Her blond friend scoffs. "She's too plain. No, he'll find her amusing for a time, then cast her aside like all the others."

Nicolas stiffens.

"But their majesties—"

"It doesn't matter. The Council will never approve the match. Everyone knows Lady Serafina owns the Council, and she wants an alliance with Linaria. The king and queen don't dare go against the Council."

My ears perk up at the information. There was no Lady Serafina at the party or in the records the Godmothers gave me. I file the tidbit away to examine later when I'm not trapped in a hedge.

The youngest woman delicately frowns, her forehead crinkling. "The king and queen might overrule the Council. They seem intent on him making a love match."

She of the towering hair flaps her hands. "You're such a dear. The prince is too busy running around to pay Princess Aryanna any attention. Besides, if all he wants is a tumble, I'm sure that peasant brat of his is more than willing."

The prince growls under his breath, the hot air tickling my cheek.

The woman on the bench stands, sending her hat into a jingling frenzy. "Let's go back to the party. The queen will want to hear all about the supper I'm throwing for that Cabriaren guttersnipe. Of course, they won't appreciate the hours I'll spend on it." She sniffs.

The blond woman says, "Queen Renata and that princess wouldn't know good taste if it bit them on their backsides. The queen would be more at home gutting pigs than at a supper party."

Uh-oh. I clamp my hand over Nicolas's mouth and wrap my other arm around him, digging my heels into the dirt. He writhes against me, but I keep my hold until the women are out of sight.

He stomps out of the hedge. "Those—those—those—*arrrgh*! Why did you stop me?" He paces the length of the small garden.

I have no idea. I was going on instinct. "We couldn't let them find us in a hedge together. Think of the scandal." *Whew, that sounds reasonable.*

"How could you just stand there while they spewed that vitriol about my mother? And you? I wanted to wring their necks."

I shrug as I settle on the bench. The feeble slurs from the women hardly measure up against all the insults the Godmothers have thrown at me over the years. It's more interesting that Nicolas is so affected by them. "Surely you're used to people insulting you."

He looks dumbfounded as he stumbles to a stop in front of me. "No."

Huh. I thought royalty would be sophisticated and thick-skinned, but in some ways, Nicolas has led a much gentler life. His innocence is … endearing.

I shake my head. *There I go, romanticizing him.* "There's no point in arguing with people like that."

"But—but—you heard them. They hate you."

I shrug. "Why are you here? I thought this was only for the noblewomen."

"No reason, just passing by," he says innocently.

Too innocently. "Don't tell me the Floren prince has nothing scheduled? Gaia has my every minute between now and the end of the century planned. She's even calculated how many seconds I can chew each bite at supper."

Nicolas grins. "Ah, that Gaia. She's a sharp one. But don't let her deceive you, she's a cream bun underneath. If she likes you, you can get away with anything."

How does he know that? Gaia is part of the entourage hired to come with me to Floren. And even if he's friendly with the servants, it's not like there are a lot of opportunities for their paths to cross.

I keep my tone light. "Do you know her?"

"Who?"

"Gaia. She's filling in for Lady Vivia until my companion recovers."

"How would I know one of your staff?"

How indeed ...

He pulls me up from the bench. "Come on, I need a distraction before I go dunk those annoying women in a fountain."

"I should return to the party ..." But I hesitate.

Playing nice with the nobles is dreadfully boring. It's wearying being the center of everyone's attention. Unnatural. I don't know how Nicolas and his parents tolerate it. Mayhap it's different if you're born into it.

Nicolas grins. "I'm afraid you can't."

"Your mother wouldn't approve of me leaving so early."

"On the contrary, she's the one who ordered me to whisk

you away."

I narrow my eyes. "Your mother. The queen. Wants me to abandon a party given in my honor. To go off. Unchaperoned. With you."

"Yes." He puts his hands in his pockets and rocks back on his heels, smile growing broader by the second.

Amusement bubbles up. *He's incorrigible.* Playful antics aside, this is the perfect opportunity to find out if the prince knows what's going on or can point me to people who do. *Really, it's my duty to go with him.*

But not dressed like this.

"Turn around." When he hesitates, I make a spinning motion with my hand.

He crinkles his forehead but follows my instructions.

"Don't look."

I wait to ensure he won't peek, then pull up my skirt and yank the two extra underskirts off. The hat and gloves quickly follow. *Ahhh, so much better.* I grab the bundle and stuff it into the hedge.

Nicolas, acting the gentleman for once, keeps his eyes straight ahead despite all the noise I'm making. *It's a good thing I'm not an assassin.* No witnesses, no way for anyone to know we're alone in the garden together. He really needs to have more care for his safety. Or, if he won't, the palace guards should.

"I'm ready."

The prince spins around. "Wonderful, now—"

"Nicolas!" A sharp voice cuts through the air on the other side of the hedge. "You have a *package* waiting."

A groan escapes my lips. *What's the girl from the woods doing here?*

His friend rounds the corner of the shrubbery, her fiery

red hair a bright splash of color in the winter landscape. Unfortunately, her hair isn't the only attractive thing about her. Her brown eyes and lightly freckled nose are a nice counterbalance to her high cheekbones and heart-shaped face. She may be slim, but I can see the defined muscles in her arms.

When she spots me, she stops and smirks. "Well, well, well. If it isn't your little lynx from the woods. I didn't know you were collecting strays."

I bare my canines at her. "You should watch out for strays. They bite."

"Don't worry, I can put down any that run across my path." She pats the dagger on her hip.

"Strays have claws of their own. And they're not afraid to fight."

Nicolas clears his throat. "Ladies. Allow me to make the introductions."

She makes a dismissive gesture. "The Cabriaren princess, I've heard."

"Nicolas never bothered to mention you." My stomach twists. *That was mean.* Ten seconds around her, and all my training goes out the window. I want to take back the words, but it's too late.

Nicolas's face hardens. "Her name is Lia."

I muster up a smile—tight, but as genuine as I can make it. "Pleased to meet you, Lia." I dip into a curtsy.

She snorts and cracks her knuckles. "Nicolas, we need to leave. Now."

"Right." He bows stiffly to me. "Princess."

They walk off together, whispering, neither sparing a glance back at me.

With a sigh, I plop down on the bench, sternly telling

myself I'll go back to the ice party in five minutes.

My spying foray didn't go well. I can't carry on a conversation without appearing like a dullard. I alienated Nicolas by rising to Lia's bait. One little snide comment, and I turn into a snarky brat. I thought I was well prepared for my role in overthrowing the royal family, but every minute I become more painfully aware of how woefully inadequate my skills are.

Going back to the celebration requires a new plan. Letting the ladies chat endlessly about fashion or sheep or the next entertainment is fine and good, but it won't help me learn who to neutralize when the Godmothers make their move. *I need to steer the conversation to topics that will be useful, without raising suspicions. Asking about the disappearing prisoners and supplies would be too blunt. Something subtler ...*

The five-minute mark passes. Then the ten. Fifteen.

Gaia limps into the sunken garden. "There you are. You need to change before you meet the queen in her solarium." She pauses. "Are you well, sweetling? Did something happen at the party?"

I give her a bright smile. "Everything is fine. I just wanted to catch my breath for a minute."

She sits next to me and puts her arm around me, her hand rubbing my arm. I stiffen—then force my muscles to relax. Being touched makes me uncomfortable, but a princess would appreciate the comforting gesture. *Don't squirm.*

"This must be hard on you. So many expectations. Surrounded by strangers in a strange place."

I shrug one shoulder. "It's all part of being a princess."

"Being a princess doesn't mean you aren't a person.

Don't be afraid to ask for what you need." She nods firmly. "It's decided. You're too tired to attend the queen this afternoon. Why don't you visit the library, or the stables, or try the hedge maze?"

I grin, remembering Nicolas's comment about the hedge maze only being fit for ladies. "Really, I'm fine. I'd like to spend time with the queen." The more time I'm around her, the more likely cracks will appear in that kindhearted disguise. Surely she's not as nice as she appears to be.

She stands and offers me a hand up. "Then let's get you ready."

My second chance. I better not blow it.

10

The queen's solarium may be huge, but the number of ladies and accompanying perfume cloud make it claustrophobic. There's not an empty seat in the room. Women drape on settees, chairs, and couches scattered in the space and lining the wall of windows overlooking the gardens. The spaces between the furniture are barely wide enough for the servers to squeeze through. A few women linger around the edges with disgruntled expressions as they wait for footmen to bring in more chairs.

From what I've inferred from the queen's subtle comments, they're the normal desperate toadies looking to gain favors and influence. Most of them stop by and chat with the queen, throwing a few comments my way to test my openness to their advances. Thank the heavens Queen Renata reserved the couch for her and me alone, otherwise some of them would try to sit in my lap.

Queen Renata smoothly sends another courtier on their way, giving us a few moments of peace before the next lady descends.

The queen produces a piece of embroidery from the basket at her side and pushes it into my hands. "Quick, if we look busy, they might leave us alone." She grabs another bundle and shakes it out, revealing a tunic.

Is she ... mending?

The queen's needle flies through the fabric with smooth, even strokes that put my clumsy attempts to shame. "If you need a rest, please feel free to excuse yourself. There's a few more guests here than I was expecting." She gives me a wry smile.

Bold souls to come without an invitation. Or foolish. The disregard for protocol would throw Godmother Twelve into a cold fury, but the queen only seems amused.

The thought of the Godmother reminds me I'm neglecting my duties. "Are Lady Rosamund and Lady Elisabetta joining us?" Now that they believe my head is full of fluff, mayhap they'll let their guard down.

"They're too intelligent to get trapped with this crowd. And as happy as I am to spend more time with you, I was trying to spare you the same fate. Didn't Nicolas find you in the gardens?"

Unfortunately. I seem to be an expert at doing the wrong thing around him. I shouldn't have lost my temper with Lia, but I also shouldn't be this bothered by it. Or by Nicolas's reaction. I'm letting things get too personal. Right after this I'll apologize to Lia and Nicolas, if only to repair the damage and put them at ease so they won't make my life difficult. But really, I need to apologize so my conscious will quiet down.

What should I tell the queen? Obviously, Nicolas hasn't said anything to her ... yet. "Was he supposed to find me?" I ask innocently. *Better to leave it vague than confess he left me.*

"Hmm. I wonder what kept him." The queen ties off the stitch, then starts on another patch. "Aryanna, will your parents join us for the ball?"

My hand freezes. *The Cabriare king and queen are coming here? They'll expose me as an imposter. Do the Godmothers know they're coming?* I swallow hard. *If only Vivia wasn't ill, she could warn them.* "I'm not sure."

"I hope they do. It's been too long since I've seen Julianna."

I wince as the needle stabs my finger. "You know the—um, my mother?"

"Oh yes, we spent summers together but lost touch for several years. She never told you?" Queen Renata frowns. "I do hope you and Nicolas realize we're not trying to pressure you into anything. We want you both to be happy. Your mother and I have love matches, and we wouldn't want anything less for you and Nicolas. Ruling a kingdom is hard enough. Your partner should share your burden, not add to it." The queen shakes her head. "There I go, prattling on. Why don't you sneak out of here and—"

The door to the solarium is thrown open, catching everyone's attention.

Godmother Twelve strides in.

11

Godmother Twelve. My heart stops. *Is it time? Is this the signal? I don't have any of my weapons! I can't even find them.* Wherever Eight—I mean Vivia—concealed them, she did too good a job.

The queen stands and holds out her arms. "Lady Serafina, I'm so pleased you're home. We weren't expecting you for another month."

What!

Godmother Twelve kisses the queen on both cheeks. "We ran into a storm near Aemilia and had to turn around. Wonderful to see you again, Princess Aryanna." She gives me a perfunctory curtsy, her amber eyes boring into my blue ones.

"Y-yes." I incline my head. "I'm delighted you've returned safely."

Godmother Twelve watches me a beat longer, then turns back to the queen. "I have urgent business to discuss with you."

A mantle of seriousness drops on Queen Renata's

shoulders in the blink of an eye. "Let's adjourn to the green parlor. I'll have someone fetch Luka."

"No need to bother the king yet." Godmother Twelve nods to me, her eyes narrowing over her beaklike nose. "I'll speak with you again soon, Princess."

Is that a warning? I keep my face impassive as my insides turn to water. *What does she know? Will she blame me for Vivia's illness? Demand an explanation for how I've mangled things so far? If she finds out Nicolas knows I can fight—* My toes curl in my slippers. "I look forward to it."

The queen and Godmother Twelve leave. A few ladies are thoughtless enough to rush after them but stop in their tracks at the Godmother's frosty glare.

Without my protector, the women descend on me in a wave and chatter around me. I replay the Godmother's words and make vague sounds as the conversation flows my direction.

Godmother Twelve is Lady Serafina, a Council member and clearly a close advisor to their majesties. The Cabriare envoy too? She made it sound like she knows Princess Aryanna. Why didn't she tell me? She knows the king and queen! No wonder she was able to arrange Princess Aryanna's visit and my subsequent substitution. I knew she was clever, but this is incredible. She's in the perfect position to strike at Floren when our allies are ready.

So, what do the Godmothers need me for?

Gaia carries in a tray loaded with dishes as I pace around my rooms for the umpteenth time. *Where is Godmother Twelve?* I thought she'd search me out right after her meeting with the queen, but it's been hours. I'm excited to hear about her role on the Council and her plans. There's no more need for secrets between us now that Vivia is ill.

My temporary companion sets the food on the small table in the sitting room. "I'm afraid supper is canceled. Her Majesty—"

I stumble to a stop. "What happened?" An icicle lodges in my chest as I remember Godmother Twelve escorting the queen out of the solarium.

"She's fallen ill too, poor thing." Gaia wrings her hands. "A fever. It came on so suddenly. The king and prince are beside themselves."

Fevers are dangerous. And to have one come on so quickly is unusual. I bury my hands in my skirts, clenching the fabric. *Is it natural? Did Godmother Twelve do something to her?*

Gaia ushers me to the chair. "Eat, sweetling. You need your strength."

I shovel food into my mouth without tasting it as Gaia hums and fusses around the room. Godmother Twelve can't be responsible. She emphasized over and over that all the nobility was to be neutralized at the same time. The knots in my stomach loosen. It must be a normal illness. *A fever. I know how to treat fevers.* And getting the queen help soon, before the illness has time to rob her of her strength, is critical.

Should I help her? Will the Godmothers approve? I fidget with my fork as the knots retighten. *Can I live with myself if I stand by and do nothing?*

No.

The Floren queen may be my enemy, but I don't want her hurt. *I can't hurt them—any of them.* The king and queen and Nicolas. The plan has always been to remove them from the thrones without injuring them. If I can aid the queen, I should.

For now, I'll have to make sure the Godmothers don't find out I helped Queen Renata. I don't want to hide it from them, but it would be too hard to explain, and they might misinterpret my motives. *Which means nobody can see me.*

I keep my eyes on my food and my tone casual. "Gaia, where is everyone else? The other attendants. They should help you."

"I thought you would be more comfortable without everyone fussing over you. But I am surprised there aren't more guards. I've hardly seen one in the halls. You're a princess, after all. They should take more care for your safety." She shakes her head in annoyance as she limps over to a chair and fluffs the pillow.

It's funny, I'd have thought I'd love having lots of people around to talk with after being so lonely at the villa. Instead, they're overwhelming and draining. But if it's making her duties harder ...

I bite my lip. "I don't want to be a burden."

"You're no such thing. Besides, there are plenty of hands around if I need help."

"Promise me you won't try to do everything yourself." I stand and grab her hand. "I can look after myself if you have other duties."

"I promise." She pats my hand. "But honestly, it's no hardship. You're so neat there's hardly anything to do. Now go finish up that meal before it cools." She shoos me back to the chair, then continues bustling around the room, softly singing.

Obediently I return to my seat. By the time I finish the meal, I have a plan to help the queen. It's stupid and risky and will probably end with me thrown in the dungeon.

There are a few things I need.

After Gaia leaves, I raid the closet and drawers until I come up with a simple bag and a plain dress. The lacings in the back are impossible to tie properly by myself, but a cloak thrown over my shoulders hides the sloppy job.

The king and queen's rooms probably have the items I'll need, but I won't have time to hunt around. I need to get in and out as quickly as possible without being seen. Which will be impossible because there will be doctors and maids and a thousand other people buzzing around the queen. I'll deal with that when I get there.

I wrinkle my nose against the bitter smell of the yarrow tea as I check my supplies. Strips of cloth, silk stockings, towels. A selection of other herbs and salves in case the queen has other symptoms. A skein to hold the tea. I pack everything in the bag and slip it out of sight under the cloak.

A little flame of rebellion warms the chill in my skin at what I'm about to do—if only the Godmothers knew how I was using my training. *Best not to think about it.*

I slip out my door and stride down the hallway toward the main part of the palace. The Godmothers always told me the best way to blend in is to act purposeful. The closer I get to the royal quarters, the more elaborately decorated the walls and furnishings become. My feet sink soundless into the plush carpets.

"—she looks so ill."

Two maids come hustling out of a hallway ahead carrying large baskets loaded with linens. I jump into a doorway, pressing my back against the wood.

"Hush," the other says. "You don't want anyone to panic. You know how the nobles are."

"Silly, bleating …"

Their voices fade as they turn the corner. I follow slowly, letting them get ahead of me.

Four guards stand outside the king and queen's chambers. I duck into a room at the far end of the hallway, peeking through a crack. One guard opens the door for the maids. After a few minutes, they come back out, their arms full of sheets and towels. I hold my breath as the women pass my hiding spot, but they don't glance my way.

I'll need to lure out anybody in the room and get the guards away from the door. This is going to take a really good distraction.

For the first time, I notice my surroundings and gasp. Walls and walls of books from floor to ceiling. My hands itch to grab the nearest one and start exploring—but no. The queen's need is urgent. Vowing to return later, I turn my attention to the rest of the items. The normal tables, reading chairs, and odd collections of paintings.

I grab a small oil lamp off the side table and check the door. The guards are conversing among themselves at the end of the hallway. I slip into the room across the way so I'm on the same side as the royal rooms. This one seems to be some kind of parlor for entertaining with couches, chairs, and tables, but not much in the way of decorations or curiosities. *A window—perfect.*

It's wide and tall enough for me to balance on the ledge. I lean out and survey my options. The room next door has a similar long window that's easily within reach, but there's a wide gap between that one and a balcony attached to the royal suite. It must be at least twenty feet between the second window and the balcony.

The palace wall looks to be in good shape. Burning bad luck. A neglected building is likely to have more handholds and footholds, but I'll make it work. I slip out of my cloak, dress, slippers, and stockings, then stuff them into the overly full bag.

It's a simple plan: light the oil lamp, drape a silk stocking close to the flame, and then place the lamp next to the door. In about fifteen minutes, the smoke and smell from the burning stocking will attract the guards. When they open the door to investigate, they'll knock over the lamp, breaking it and creating a small fire in the room. That'll draw anybody nearby away from the queen for a few moments—I hope.

There might be some suspicion and questions about the source of the lamp, but not enough to overly alarm them with little damage and no injuries.

Fifteen minutes to get to the queen. Four minutes to treat her and get out of the room undetected.

I dry my hands on my shift, then pull myself onto the windowsill. The wind howls, trying to pluck me off the building. I breathe deeply, calming my racing heart and my shaking hands. It's not that I'm afraid of heights. The Godmothers would never tolerate such an irrational fear, and I climbed on the roof of the villa most of my life … but that was just one level. I prefer to be on the ground is all, not dangling so high up that the people below are smudges.

Don't look down. The first steps are easy. I keep one hand on the window frame and sidle to the edge. The gap between this window and the one next door is about two feet. *Only a little step away. Simplicity itself.*

I stretch my foot out to the neighboring ledge, my toes gripping the stones. I reach across and grab hold of the wooden sill with one hand, then step across the chasm. A little wobble as I adjust my weight to the new position. *There, that was easy enough. First part down, one more to go.* My feet slide across the stone ledge as I keep my body flush with the window. My sweating hands leave streaks on the glass as I creep along the locked window. *Burning glass and burning palaces without burning balconies. Everyone loves balconies. Every window should have one.*

When I reach the far edge, I let out a small breath and scrutinize the twenty-foot section of wall that separates me from the king and queen's rooms. There's some small and large cracks that will work for footholds and handholds, but they disappear after a few feet so that's a dead end. More promising is an overhead elaborate carving of interweaving leaves and lilies that starts at the top of this window and continues across the royal suite's balcony. I can use the carvings as handholds to make it all the way to their balcony—but I won't have any footholds. I'll have to rely on my hands and arms the entire way.

I rub my hands on my smallclothes again, then rub my feet against the fabric for good measure. My toes are sluggish from the numbing cold. I cup my hands and blow on my fingers, but the heat is whipped away by the bitter wind. *It's not getting any warmer.*

My foot fits nicely into a waist-high crack. I press myself up until my fingers grasp the overhead carving. It's deep enough to provide a strong handhold. I breathe a small sigh of relief and bring up my other hand. Dangling from the carving puts the wall an inch in front of my nose. I slide my left hand to the side along the carving, then my right hand follows. *Left, right, left, right, slide, slide, slide. Don't look down. Left, right, left, right. Ignore my swinging feet.* Nerves scream I'm going to fall at any second. Sweat breaks out on my forehead.

Stone crumbles under my fingers. I slip, my right hand desperately digging into the carving. A scream sticks in my throat as my body swings away from the wall. There's only blackness around me. My toes scrabble against the wall, desperately trying to find a perch. *There!* A faint impression deep enough for my foot to push against. I throw my left hand up, fingers clawing at the wall. *Crack.* I fling myself sideways onto the balcony as a massive chunk of stone breaks away. The rock hits the ground, shattering the quiet, followed by a deafening silence.

I lie on my back and gasp at the night sky, my heart

threatening to beat out of my chest. Laughter bubbles up as my muscles turn to jelly. I long to lie on the stones for at least a day, but time's running out.

A quick peek confirms the richly decorated room is empty. *Either the diversion worked better than I hoped, or they're running an errand.* The balcony doors are locked from the inside with a simple latch. It only takes a minute to flip the lock with one of my straightened hairpins.

The queen is lying on the large curtained bed tucked against the wall. The oversized furniture makes her appear smaller, frailer. There are bright-red spots in her cheeks, and her skin looks ashy in the dim light. She's so still—my heart leaps to my throat then I see her chest rising. *I'm not too late.*

The room is stifling, thanks to the roaring fire in the fireplace. Idiots. They risk overheating the queen with her fever burning so hot. I pour water on the flames, reducing it from an inferno to a small blaze sufficient to keep the chill out of the room.

Wiping my forehead, I sit her up and dribble the yarrow tea into her mouth. She's heavier than her slim appearance would suggest. Good. Her body will have energy to use against the illness. Her eyes stay closed, and her breathing doesn't change, despite my jostling; the doctors must have drugged her to sleep. A quick massage warms up the queen's feet, then I slip wet stockings on her to draw the heat out of her body and help it fight off the infection.

I should get dressed unless I want to run around the palace in my smallclothes. But the queen stirs and makes a fretful noise, pulling me back to her side. I coax a little water between her lips while sponging her neck and forehead with a cool, damp cloth.

"What are you doing?"

Ice shoots through my veins at the angry voice. I gasp, dropping the cloth and backing away.

Nicolas is standing in the far doorway.

Muffled shouts echo through the suite.

He turns toward the noise. I grab a nearby towel and throw it over my head, racing blindly through the rooms and bursting out the doors. Two guards are standing halfway down the hallway; the others have disappeared. I dash in the opposite direction, frantically looking for a hallway or stairway to escape. A narrow door opens ahead of me. I crash into a maid, sending her a mental apology as I flee down the servants' stairway and disappear into the bowels of the palace.

What have I done?

The unforgiving sunrise stabs at my eyes as I squirm on the couch, wrapping the blanket tighter around me. I pull the fabric over my head. *Just smother me with a pillow and put me out of my misery.*

All night I waited for Nicolas to burst into my room, leading a squadron of guards to drag me to the dungeon. My mind turned every squeak in the hall into swords being drawn; every muffled voice was someone ordering my arrest. *Where in the burning are my burning daggers?* If I can't find them today, I'm going to find my way to the kitchen and steal a knife or nine. I can't survive another night without having a blade within reach.

When the door opens, I nearly jump out of my skin, falling on the floor as I tangle in the blanket. I jerk upright and yank the cover down as Gaia backs into the room with an armful of towels.

"Heavens, you're up early, sweetling. What are you doing down there? Go back to bed."

A giant yawn rises at the reminder the comfiest bed in

the world is waiting for me just steps away. "I was restless. Too many things on my mind." *Like my impending doom.*

"Your companion's condition hasn't changed, but there's one piece of good news to cheer you up. The queen is doing much better. She's resting this morning but is expected to join the court for supper." She looks around as though checking that we're alone. "I heard from her maids the queen threw a right fit when the doctors tried to dose her today. Fairly tossed them out on her ears." Gaia chuckles. "She's someone I would never cross."

That news is more welcome than Gaia realizes. As happy as I am that the queen is getting better, her recovery also means there's a slim chance I can stay out of the dungeon after all. Her fever must have been less severe than they originally suspected. The doctors likely overreacted and made it worse by turning her bedroom into a furnace and pouring "cures" down her throat.

My stomach growls loud enough to startle me. Gaia laughs, then pops her head into the hallway to order a tray. I eat every bite of the delicious food as she fills me in on the other piece of good news: all my activities and events for the week are rescheduled since nobody is willing to risk the queen's health for a luncheon. Being the one blamed for her relapse would be political suicide. *The day keeps getting better and better.*

After twenty minutes of begging, pleading, and threatening, I convince Gaia I'm in desperate need of a nap and I'll sleep better alone. She tucks me into bed, promising to return midmorning.

My shoulders relax after the door closes. *Finally, time to myself.* Despite the anxious night, I'm too alert to go back to sleep. If the guards haven't come for me by now, they're never coming. And having the queen recover is icing on the bun. My mind buzzes with the need to move.

Back and arm muscles complain as I climb out of bed. Between the travel days and the unexpected turn of events at the palace, I've been neglecting my training routines. This place is so intoxicating, so seductive with its softness and comforts. I need to be careful, or I'll become as inattentive as those guards last night.

A more thoughtful foray into my closet yields one of the tunic and legging sets I wore at the villa for some of my more distasteful chores. I go through the sword poses I've been doing since I could walk, controlling my breathing as I move through the series in graceful, fluid movements. The familiar habit relaxes my mind and centers me in a way I haven't felt since my arrival.

In the middle of pose thirteen, Nicolas strolls in without knocking, an oversized hat with a long black feather perched jauntily on his head.

"Good morning, my little lynx." He pauses midstep, seemingly surprised to find me in the sitting room with the furniture pushed back against the walls. His gaze travels from the top of my braided hair, down the unconventional clothing, and lands on my bare feet. "Not your typical princess sleepwear."

I bristle. "And how would you know?"

"A gentleman never kisses and tells."

"Then I'm sure I'll be hearing all about your exploits." His laugh echoes across the room.

A warmth blooms in my chest at his delighted grin. I give myself a mental smack. Just because I enjoy matching wits with him, it means nothing. It's just he's not what I expected from a prince. "Why are you here?"

"To see you, of course."

"I thought you were mad at me?"

"You, my little lynx? Never."

At my arched eyebrow, the playful manner falls away. He straightens and fixes me with a penetrating look. "I know that was you last night."

I fight to keep my face immobile. "I don't know what you're talking about."

He snorts. "I was ready to strangle you when I found out about that fire trap you set for the guards. What were you thinking?"

Seemed like a great diversion at the time. And it was. "Why didn't you?"

He wanders to the writing desk and picks up a piece of stationery. "After the fire was out, I checked on my mother. Mia—the maid you tried to trample—was excited about the wonderful new treatments the doctors were trying and how well she was already responding."

I bite the inside of my cheek. Nicolas folds the paper, then folds it again, his eyes trained on me.

What is he thinking? This serious Nicolas is hard to read. Does he believe I was trying quaint, folksy remedies, and no harm was done? Is he angry for interfering with the doctors?

He bows. "Thank you for helping my mother."

I look away, twisting my fingers in the hem of my shirt. It's easier to deal with him when he's making jokes and being playful, not expressing gratitude and looking vulnerable. "Your mother deserves the credit. Or the doctors."

He walks over. "Say you're welcome." He kisses the back of my hand.

Heat fills my cheeks. I tilt my chin up and give him a

sassy grin, trying to get us back to safer ground. "You're welcome."

The air sizzles between us as Nicolas gazes at me with those intense gray eyes. I desperately want to break the moment, but the words won't form. I don't want to think too hard about why my heart is fluttering.

His eyes darken from silver to smoke. "You're not at all what I expected."

"What was that?"

"The normal spoiled, silly princess who's more interested in court gossip than what's happening in the kingdom. My parents are quite impressed with you."

My breath catches. "But you aren't?"

"I'm keeping an open mind. You're clever. Charming. And beautiful, of course. But I have to ask myself why a princess can fight like you can. Why she would sneak into the queen's room instead of demanding access. And in her smallclothes, no less. You're a mystery."

Oh. A mix of pleasure and disappointment swirls through me. I thought I was doing so well playing a princess, but I'm not deceiving anyone.

"Let's start over." He straightens and offers his hand. "Nicolas of Floren. I enjoy spying on foreign delegations in the woods and eating maritozzi until I'm sick."

"Pleased to meet you." I take his hand and dip into a curtsy. "Aryanna of Cabriare. I enjoy attacking strangers with tree branches and hiding in hedges during garden parties."

"Hiding in hedges? I'm intrigued. I've never met a princess with that particular hobby. You'll have to show me how it's done. There's too many boring garden parties I've been forced to sit through because I didn't know hiding in the hedge was an option."

"Oh, it's quite useful, I assure you. More practical in summer than winter, of course. And there's a certain skill level required to avoid getting impaled on a branch or entangled in greenery, but I'm sure you'll master it in no time."

"Mayhap you can demonstrate this marvelous talent for me soon."

He's still holding my hand. Why is he still holding my hand? I shouldn't be doing this. Someone could come in at any moment and see us together. *What if the Godmothers find out?*

I swallow hard and draw away, surprised by my reluctance to break our connection. He holds on, his fingers tightening for a moment as though loathe to release me. After a heartbeat, he loosens his grip and allows my hand to slide out of his. I twist my fingers behind my back. His warmth lingers on my skin.

The jovial mask falls back on his face, breaking the moment. "Where are your boots? We need to get going."

"I can't leave my room." My body tenses. *I have to stay here.*

Nicolas chuckles. "You weren't concerned with staying in your room last night. Where's the rebellious girl who tried to singlehandedly burn down the palace?"

My nails dig into my palms. "That was different."

But why? Why can't I leave my room? Gaia's suggested I explore the palace several times, but I've always refused. Why am I so reluctant to go anywhere?

It's not the people. It's been nice hearing them chatter and laugh around the palace. Nobody stopped me last night when I was roaming through the palace. And I had no trouble chasing Nicolas through the woods.

This isn't the villa.

Here, I'm a princess. I can go anywhere I want, ask for anything. Nobody will stop me. *So why am I stopping myself?*

He disappears into my closet, whistling a jaunty tune.

"Hey, you can't go in there!"

His reply is too muffled to make out.

I sigh and rub my temples. *The boy has no sense of propriety.*

I sit on the couch and help myself to the sticky buns Gaia left cooling. Random exclamations and shouts come from the closet. I'm licking the last of the honey off my fingers when he finally emerges with a triumphant yell, boots in hand.

"Success!"

"Finally found them at the front of the closet?"

He brushes off my sarcasm. "I can't believe the mess in there. You should fire your maid."

I cross my arms. "Gaia does a wonderful job taking care of me."

He holds up his hands to ward off my rebuke. "Just a joke, Lady Lynx." He pulls a crumpled wad of fabric out of his pocket and reaches for my foot.

"*Signore!*" I yank my feet out of his reach and give him a withering look. "You cannot take such liberties."

He chuckles as he reaches out again. "No time for modesty, we're late."

I scramble off the couch.

We stare at each other, a silent war of wills.

He sighs. "Fine. But I'll drag you out if you're not ready in two minutes." He tosses the fabric on the couch and strolls whistling out of the room.

I wait until the door closes before picking it up. The bundle is deceptively soft and fuzzy. It takes a moment to puzzle out they're an odd form of stockings. Much shorter and thicker than the silk ones I've been wearing at the palace. I pull them on, admiring the subtle leaf pattern woven into the fabric.

My head shoots up at the sound of someone clearing their throat.

Nicolas stands in the doorway. "One minute." He winks, then steps outside.

My feet are wonderfully warm as I yank on my boots and a second shirt to protect against the chill. I toy for a moment with staying inside the room. *Would he really drag me out? Judging by the mischief so far, undoubtedly.* Shaking my head, I open the door.

My heart skips a beat as he grabs my hand and pulls me down the empty hallway. My hand fits perfectly in his.

"Nicolas, I can't go out like this." I try to pull away, but his grip is strong … and I don't fight that hard. "There'll be gossip."

"Of course, the princess can't be seen in trousers. Think of the scandal." He sweeps off his broad hat and plops it on my head, tipping it down over my eyes. "Come along, squire."

I push the brim up so I can squint at him. "Squire? You can't seriously think people will believe that."

"People believe whatever they want to believe. And we're off."

He tows me along as I laugh, waving hello to the nobles and servants we pass in the halls. Despite being close in height, I have to trot to keep up with his longer strides.

Nicolas pauses by the front doors, where a woman with dimples and curly black hair streaked with gray is holding two thick cloaks.

He takes them from her and kisses her on the cheek. "Carmella, my love! When are you going to run away with me?"

She pats his cheek as she chuckles. "Stop trying to turn my head, you rogue. Flirting with me in front of your friend." She turns her gaze to me. "Don't mind our prince. He just wants to see an old woman smile."

I lean in and whisper loud enough for Nicolas to hear, "I don't know, he seems rather incorrigible. Any advice for dealing with him?"

He pretends to be wounded while she laughs. "You're doing just fine, dear." She turns back to the prince. "Your mother is expecting you both for supper. Make sure you don't disappoint her."

"Then we better hurry. Come on, my little lynx." Nicolas drops a cloak into my arms then throws open the doors, striding out into the cold.

Carmella stops me before I follow him. "He really is a good lad." She looks like she's making up her mind about something, then adds, "Nicolas doesn't want you to know it, but he wasn't happy when his parents issued you an invitation to visit. He knows they expect you two to marry. But everything changed once he met you. I've never seen him happier. Give him a chance."

Her confession surprises me. "I hope he'll give me one. I don't really know him."

"He wouldn't tease you if he didn't like you." Carmella touches my arm. "Give it time. Nobody's expecting either of you to jump into anything, including the king and queen."

I give her a noncommittal smile, then slip out the door to find Nicolas waiting by two saddled horses.

I tuck my braid up into my hat and look him over. "Don't you need a disguise too?"

"My astonishing good looks will prevent people from recognizing me. But you're right, I wouldn't want anyone to go blind staring at me." He calls out to one of the hostlers, tossing the man a silver coin in exchange for his misshapen hat.

I shake my head—*he can't believe we're actually tricking anyone. They'd have to be blind, deaf, and dumb to be misled by our poor disguises.* While Nicolas checks the tack on the dappled gelding, I make friends with the sweet mare with the red coat and a white forelock, then swing into the saddle.

Nicolas bursts into laughter.

I look around, trying to find the source of his amusement until I realize it's me. "What?"

"I don't know why you always manage to surprise me. Of course you can mount without assistance and ride astride. And you think I'm scandalous."

I roll my eyes. "It would look rather odd for your *squire* to ride sidesaddle."

He continues chuckling as he mounts his horse, then trots out the gates.

The sight of the stone archway fills me with hesitation. *Should I turn around? Go back? What would Godmother Twelve say?*

Godmother Twelve wanted me to stay away from Nicolas, but things have changed. She hasn't come to see me, even though she's surely heard of Godmother Eight's illness by now. And mayhap I'll find something in the city to settle the growing uneasiness I feel every time I compare the Godmothers' tales to the people I've met. There must be a reason the Godmothers say the nobility is corrupt, and I need to find it.

My pulse thrums as I picture riding outside the palace. Nobody will chase after me. Nobody will punish me for daring to dream of the world outside my walls. Tears prick in my eyes; I quickly wipe them away on my sleeve.

Nicolas pauses outside the gate. He rears his horse and waves an arm, shouting, "The city awaits!"

I nudge my horse and walk it forward, holding my breath as I pass through the gate. I look up, clutching the hat. The sun dazzles my eyes. A smile spreads across my face and I laugh, every nerve tingling with excitement.

Nicolas watches me with a puzzled look on his face as I trot over to him.

"Where to first?" I ask breathlessly.

14

I dawdle on the road, trying to memorize every moment. Nicolas doesn't let me linger too long, promising that the marketplace is worth the hurry. It doesn't disappoint.

The glorious smells perfuming the air are the first hint we're getting closer. Roasted meats and spices tease the nose, filling my mind with images of food until the noise distracts me. At first, it's a dull roar of jumbled sounds. Occasionally a word or drumbeat escapes the symphony to rise above and demand my attention. As we get closer, the sounds become more distinct: vendors pushing their merchandise, people haggling over prices, snatches of music from the street performers, laughter and conversation between the patrons. We turn a corner, and the full marketplace comes into view.

The small glimpse I got from the carriage window didn't do it justice.

It's an explosion of colors. Clothing, canopies, people, animals—everything is bright and new. I could spend the rest of my life here and never see it all. The people are even more fascinating than the wares. Skin of soft moonlight to midnight black, and everything in between. And their clothing! Sleeves sweeping to the ground, bared stomachs, lacings on trousers, heeled boots, thin slippers. It's like the entire world has descended on Floren to barter.

Every inch of the market is something new to look at, another thing to wonder and exclaim over. I should try to keep a scrap of dignity, but I can't help gasping every few seconds. Nicolas has a bemused expression on his face as I drag him from stall to stall.

After the twentieth vendor, he pulls me to the side and hands me a heavy purse of coins. "Make sure you overpay a little. It's good for the merchants, and we can afford to share the wealth."

I grip the bag with both hands. He … wants me to purchase things … with his money. *Is this a test?* "What should I buy?"

"Whatever you want, Lady Lynx." He tilts his head, his brow furrowing. "Haven't you shopped in a market before?"

Should I tell him the truth or play the sophisticate? Color stains my cheeks. I don't know why the thought of admitting this is so embarrassing. "I don't need anything."

I try to give him the coins, but he pushes them back into my hands. "The market is more exciting when you can shop. You'll figure it out in no time."

I desperately want to try my hand at it. This place is fascinating. To buy one of the gorgeous baubles spread out on the tables would be incredible. And not only that, I could talk with the people. Strangers who won't know who I am. People who can't possibly carry tales about me to the Godmothers. Here, I'm just another face in the crowd, nobody remarkable.

The bands around my chest release. I take a deep, cleansing breath. *Freedom.*

I give Nicolas a shy smile. "Could you show me how to do it?"

The prince looks pleased. "I'd be happy to."

He has me eavesdrop on a housewife bargaining over flour so I can see how it's done. Then he points me toward a stall I've been eyeing, piled high with fruits and vegetables, while he wanders a few feet away.

The table has a mix of the familiar and the exotic. Grapes, lemons, and carrots sit side-by-side with other produce I can only guess at. My stomach jumps as I catch the attention of the owner and start haggling. Minutes later I walk away clutching a net bag of oranges and a pot filled with tiny purple berries, and I am positively drunk on excitement and power.

I thrust my purchases into his face. "Look! I bought these. It was just like the woman. He offered a price, and I countered, and we went back and forth and back and forth until we agreed, and then I gave him the money, and he gave them to me. I can't believe it!"

"You did it." Nicolas picks me up and spins me around. "You were magnificent."

My breath comes faster as he slowly lowers me to the ground, his strong hands wrapped around my waist. His eyes dart to my mouth, and I lick my lips, nervous at what might—or might not—happen. I want him to kiss me. Badly. *This is my enemy.* But he doesn't seem like a bad person. The opposite, in fact.

Someone jostles me. I stumble to the side, shattering the moment.

Nicolas offers to take my purchases to where we've

stabled the horses, so I won't have to carry them around the market. I'm loathe to let my prizes out of my sight, but it would be awkward to keep a hold of them, especially if I find something else to buy. My eyes linger on his broad shoulders and confident step as he weaves through the crowd.

What am I doing? I'm supposed to be learning about him, not flirting. It'd be one thing if it was an act, but my emotions are getting involved, confusing me. Just because he seems nice doesn't mean he is. Evil can wear many faces. Every precaution must be taken until I find out who the real enemy is. And even if my heart insists it can't possibly be Nicolas, right now I need to listen to my head.

It's unlikely I'll find any answers today. The few people who seem to recognize the prince have limited themselves to nods and smiles. Nobody looked like they were waiting for an opportunity to approach him. Instead of hunting out conspiracies, I decide to lose myself in the marketplace. I take my time browsing through rolls of fabric, potted meats and jellies, sparkling glass, and a tinker's odd assortment of goods. At a stall selling perfumes, a pair of young lovers laughing over a shared joke. They seem so carefree, like the only thing that matters in the world is the other person.

Where's Nicolas? It shouldn't take this long to drop my purchases off. Mayhap he's having trouble finding me in the throng. I edge my way through the crowd, scanning faces as I go.

I spot Nicolas standing at the entrance of an alley and shrug away the nagging thought that I shouldn't be able to recognize him at this distance. As I make my way in his direction, the crowd parts for a moment, revealing a short redhead chatting with him, their heads close together, her hand on his arm.

My steps stutter to a stop, and I shiver at the sudden drop in temperature. I'd recognize that hair anywhere—the girl from the woods. Lia. A small jab of jealousy runs through me, but I smash it down. The prince isn't mine to claim, not really. He's free to talk to whoever he wants to. He doesn't owe me anything.

I turn away, pulling my cloak tighter around my shoulders. I randomly wander over to a booth with fluttering crimson streamers. Sunlight glints off the steel pieces placed around the table on a black velvet covering. A spark of interest grows as I examine the weapons on display. These are quality pieces: exquisite folding on the blades, and hilts designed for both beauty and grip.

"Looking for anything in particular, laddie?" The swarthy trader on the other side of the table is the first person to be conned by my thin disguise.

I drop my voice an octave, playing into the squire role. "Superb pieces." I pick up a dagger with an ebony grip. "The balance is perfect. Did you forge these yourself?"

A smile lights up his face. "Everything you see. That's one of my favorites. See the way I worked the metal?"

He launches into a detailed explanation of the techniques used to make the dagger, then snatches it and replaces it with another. I drink in the flow of words, caught up in his passion. The merchant preens under my enthusiasm and begins pulling stock from under the table to share with me. The last to emerge is a plain wooden box about the size of my two hands together.

"This," he whispers conspiratorially, "is a special project." He glances to both sides before lifting the lid.

My eyes widen. The delicate throwing knives nestled in

the velvet make all the weapons before seem clumsy and unwieldy. I reach out and gently touch one. The blades are each the length of my ring finger and look light enough to float into the air at the slightest breeze. I meet the merchant's gaze and try to say something, but the words freeze in my throat. He nods solemnly, pride shining in his eyes.

Nicolas steps up beside me. "Exquisite."

The merchant snaps the case shut and gives the prince a low bow. "Thank you, sire."

I shuffle to the side and pretend to study the daggers sitting on the far side of the table.

He says, "You must let me buy them from you. I've never seen finer craftsmanship."

"Apologies, but they're commissioned."

"Name your price, please."

"I'm truly sorry, but I wouldn't have time to replace them. I'd hate to disappoint my customer."

Nicolas's voice is heavy with disappointment. "I understand. Would you consider …"

I tune them out and look at the other nearby stalls. Red hair flashes in the crowd. I track Nicolas's companion as she slips through the market and disappears around a building. *Should I follow her?* The prince is in deep conversation with the merchant; he'll never notice if I slip away for a moment. *If I can find out why she and Nicolas were in the woods, I might be a step closer to figuring out the truth.* The reason is plausible enough that I can pretend it's the only reason I want to seek her out.

I silently curse the throng that keeps pressing in around me as I try to reach the spot where she disappeared. It takes too long to get to the building, and I stomp around the corner, expecting to find no trace of the redhead.

Instead, she's waiting for me.

15

Lia is a handbreadth shorter than me, something I use to my advantage by straightening up so I can look down on her. *What's her relationship to Nicolas? Friends? Something more?* They're comfortable with each other, judging by their easy interactions and casual touches. Obviously, I hate her.

Despite the winter air, she wears a light cloak, thin shirt, and a long brown skirt. Twin blades spin in her hands. "You again. What are you doing so far from home, little kitty?"

I narrow my eyes at the sarcasm dripping from her voice. "I didn't realize they allow field mice in town. I'll have to speak to the prince about the pest problem."

The corner of her mouth twitches into a hard smile. "I don't see any mice here."

I swallow my retort. *Temper, temper, temper. Don't say anything you'll regret again.* Lia's baiting me again and I'm falling right into her trap. "Lia, I—"

"You managed to remember my name. Congratulations, you must be so proud."

"I didn't mean to—"

"Completely embarrass yourself?"

"I'm trying to apologize for insulting you, you burning flap-fish!"

"Don't hurt yourself. I'd forgotten about you the moment Nicolas and I left you behind."

She peers behind me as the knives disappear into the folds of her cloak.

Nicolas says, "Lia, I see you're making our guest feel at home."

I frown as he slips his arm around my shoulders. I dig my elbow into his side, receiving a satisfying *oomph* for my effort, and then step out of his reach. "We were just catching up."

Nicolas glances from me to her. "I hate to interrupt, but Aryanna and I need to hurry if we want to join my parents for supper. You'll let me know when you've taken care of that issue?"

Lia gives him a saucy smile. "Of course, my prince. Anything for you. I'll deliver the message personally." She dips into an exaggerated curtsy.

Nicolas laughs. "Just make sure you're quick about it." He holds his arm out to me.

I sniff and stalk away. He catches up and whistles a tuneless melody as I dodge shoppers through the square. After a few minutes, he reaches for my arm, holding his hands up in surrender at my warning look.

"Princess," he whispers.

"What?" I snap.

"You're going the wrong the way."

Of course I am.

I sigh, then take his offered arm and wave my hand. "Lead the way."

"The city is a bit of a maze, but you'll find your way around soon enough." He leads me through the market, pointing out some of his favorite vendors as we walk.

After a minute, I jerk him to a stop. "We're walking the same direction. I wasn't going the wrong way!"

He rubs the back of his neck with a grin. "Ah, erm, yes. But how else would you to let me escort you?"

I should be mad—but I laugh. I take his arm again, shaking my head. At the stable, Nicolas tips the lad while I check the horses' tack, tightening the cinch on my saddle and untangling a knot in his reins. He sets a leisurely pace back to the palace at the top of the hill.

"I thought we were in a hurry."

"Not exactly." The prince waves to someone calling from a window overhead. "I didn't want you and Lia to kill each other before you had a chance to become friends."

I turn my snort into a cough. *Lia and me friends?* I'm more likely to run naked through the throne room than befriend that girl. And she seems more interested in stabbing me than sharing stories. No, it's safe to say friendship is not in the cards for us.

But he opened the door for me to press further into their relationship. "Is that what you two are? Friends?"

"Certainly." His face morphs into a delighted grin. "Are you jealous of Lia?"

"Course not!" But it's too late.

He gives a hearty laugh, slapping his thigh and startling his horse.

I tilt my nose into the air and look away. Let him think what he wants. Sure, her hair and features might appeal to some boys, but obviously she can't be trusted. As like to cut someone as to kiss them. Actually, she's definitely more likely to cut them. Nicolas included.

The flash of anger that comes with picturing Lia kissing Nicolas gets shoved down as quickly as it reared up. Giving him my best condescending look, I ask, "Are you quite finished?"

"Almost." His guffaws die down to mere chuckles. "I met Lia years ago. We're friends. *Only* friends." He looks at me to ensure I understand.

He could be lying—but I want to believe him. And he did flirt with me in front of her. That would be very strange if there were romantic feelings between them. Lia was just trying to get under my skin.

I pat my mare's neck. "You seem to have a habit of attracting women who like knives."

"Why, Lady Lynx, are you admitting you've fallen for my charms? Just say the word, and I'll sweep you off your feet."

"The only way you're sweeping me off my feet is with a kick spin."

"And that's why I love women who love daggers. Any other girl would fawn all over me. But you won't fall for shallow compliments and pretty baubles."

"Don't count on it. Those wares at the marketplace were plenty pretty. I might get it in my head to run off with one of those stall owners if he promises to keep me in daggers and ribbons."

Nicolas groans. "I knew you were eyeing that weapons dealer. I'll have to challenge him to a duel for your love."

I playfully shake my head. "Killing an artist like that would not ingratiate yourself to me. No, that's not the way to my heart."

"Then what must I do, fair maiden? Shall I go to the

ends of the earth for a rare flower? Pluck the moon from the night sky? Tell me what you desire, and it will be yours."

"Oh, good sir, all I need are the stars in your eyes." I flutter my lashes at him.

We burst into laughter, the people walking in the street shooting us amused looks.

Nicolas pulls his horse to a stop as the palace gates come into view. "Will you be joining us for supper?"

I toy with the reins, running the leather strips through my fingers. "I don't want to impose."

"There's no imposition. My mother would be delighted to see you. Father too."

I want to ask him if he wants me to come, but I fear the answer. And what I want him to say. "I guess I can suffer with your company if it means I get to enjoy theirs."

He chuckles and shakes his head. "Women who love daggers ..."

The cheery fire crackles, the light reflecting off the tiles we're using to play something called Wolves and Rivers. Heat and wisps of escaped wood smoke drift through the room. Seeing the Floren royal family splayed out on the floor of the parlor would likely come as a shock to most of the nobility, but when the queen suggested we sit in front of the fire to finish our after-dinner tea, it seemed like the most natural move in the world.

King Luka says, "I wager two almonds." He tosses the nuts into the small pile in the center of the red-and-gold carpet.

Queen Renata glances at my tiles, then whispers, "Raise him five. Luka can't resist a challenge." She raises her voice. "Nicolas, are you almost done? Your father is stealing your almonds when he thinks we're not looking."

I smother my giggles as the king snatches his hand back from the abandoned pile of nuts, pretending to look wounded. "If you'd let me have that second helping of cake, I wouldn't be forced to scavenge for food."

"You had two pieces. Order something from the kitchens if you're so hungry."

"But it's so much more fun to take his." He grins at his wife as he grabs another handful of almonds from the prince's pile.

She laughs, the firelight teasing out red highlights in her black braids. "Nicolas?"

The prince waves from the corner, where he's hunched over a small table. "Just one more moment. That spring I picked up in the marketplace needed a few adjustments." He exchanges the small hammer in his hand for a pair of clippers.

I ask the queen, "What's he working on?"

"I never know. He likes to surprise us with his inventions."

He's full of surprises. "What does he make?"

"Almost anything as long as it has moving parts. He shows us the trinkets and amusements. A carriage he made for the cook's daughter. Carved knights with moving arms and legs that he gave to the younger lads in the stable."

King Luka says, "It's the ones he doesn't tell us about that are especially remarkable. Like how he helped fix the fountain in the lower district. Even reworked the pump so now it feeds a little trough for animals. The master engineer said it was a brilliant design." His eyes glow with pride as he strokes his black-and-silver beard.

Queen Renata looks at her son with a fond smile. "He's always happiest when he's building things."

Nicolas straightens with a triumphant noise. "It's ready."

The odd contraption he sets in front of the fireplace is certainly eye-catching. On top of a little round base sits a figurine of a man and women in mid-dance with a few lifelike bushes scattered around them. Lightly painted glass panes in blue, green, and red are attached to the edges.

He winds a small crank, then releases it. The dancers slowly spin in a circle, and I can almost hear the music playing. Firelight catches the coated panels, casting moving colored shadows on the walls.

I've never seen anything like it. *To think Nicolas built this with his own two hands!* I'd never paid any special attention to his fingers before, but now I find myself staring at them. Strong, flexible. Callouses from handling weapons and riding. A scar on his right thumb that I don't know the story behind, but I want to.

The king leans closer and studies the device. "Fascinating. This would create a bidding war in the marketplace. Every noble in the kingdom would desire it for bragging rights."

The queen claps her hands together. "It's marvelous, darling. Wherever did you get the idea for it?"

Nicolas looks at me. "I was inspired by something I saw in the woods."

Heat rushes into my cheeks and look down at my lap.

He says, "I'm planning on giving it to Tonio for Elena."

For an instant, I'm disappointed. But imagining the little girl's excitement as her father gives her such a fantastical gift makes the present even more special. As much as I'd like to keep the device for myself, I want her to have it so much more. "I think she'll love it."

Nicolas and I share a smile.

Queen Renata says, "That's wonderfully kind of you. She's had such a hard year after losing her mother last winter. But I'm glad we have the chance to enjoy it tonight." She gathers the tiles scattered on the carpet. "Let's play another round. And this time, Luka, no cheating. I saw you trying to slip that piece under your foot."

"My heart, you wound me! I would never be so clumsy as to cheat so that you could catch me." The king puts his hand behind his back and furtively shows me the tile in his palm. "You're going to have our guest thinking the worst of me."

His mother says, "The heavens will never strike me down for telling the truth, my love. A wonderful king you may be, but also a terrible player."

Nicolas chuckles. "The worst in the kingdom."

King Luka hangs his head in feigned shame. "It's true, Aryanna. Don't tell your parents. If your father ever hears how often I lose to my wife and son, I'd have to stop all trade between our kingdoms for fear of my humiliation spreading."

I place my hand over my heart. "Your secret is safe with me."

"I knew I could count on you." He slyly passes me the stolen tile with a conspiratorial wink as the queen pretends not to notice. "Now, whose turn is it to go first?"

I yawn as I look at my reflection in the polished disc at my dressing table. Gaia's gentle hands work their magic on my hair, unpinning the tresses and brushing them out. Her ministrations are hypnotic, and I find myself lulled toward sleep.

"Gaia …" I pause. What do I want to say? My day has been one of extremes, with Nicolas teasing me mercilessly one moment and driving me to blush at his thoughtfulness in the next. He seems to be full of contradictions. I thought the prince of Floren would be wrapped up in parties and gossip and extremes, but the closest he came to gossip was a hilarious story about an uppity noble tripping into a duck pond. Despite our short time together, it's like I've known him for years.

I catch Gaia's bemused expression in the mirror and give her a weak smile. "I'm sorry for keeping you up late. You should go to bed."

"Nonsense, I want to hear about your day. It was quiet here. Prince Nicolas disappeared early this morning and wasn't seen again until supper. And you, poor thing, were resting all day." She gives me a conspiratorial smile.

Gaia is another mystery. She should scold me for vanishing from my rooms and spending the day unchaperoned with the prince. Instead, she created a cover story and seems delighted I misbehaved. Somehow, she sneaked under my defenses and became my friend without my noticing.

"It was … interesting. Nicolas isn't at all what I expected. He's so … happy. And he makes everyone around him happy too." I remember how Nicolas flirted with the maid this morning, making her smile. And not just her; everyone seems to smile more when Nicolas is around.

"And he's handsome."

I snort. "And he knows it. Handsome is fine and good, but I'd rather find someone I can talk to."

"Is the prince so boring?"

Things would be a lot simpler if he were. "He has a quick wit and seems knowledgeable, at least about his kingdom. He makes me laugh." My thoughts stray to the conversation with Lia. "But he's hiding something." I snap my mouth shut. I must be more tired than I thought, to be so careless.

Her hands are still in my hair. "What do you think he's hiding?"

I force out a little trill. "Nothing, I'm just being silly. I've only known him a few days. How could I possibly know if he's hiding something? And even so, a person's entitled to a few secrets."

Gaia returns to braiding my hair. "Of course, sweetling. Part of the fun of getting to know someone is when they choose to share those secrets with you."

She hums as she ties off the loose braid with a ribbon, then tucks me into bed with a glass of honeyed milk.

After she leaves, I mull over her words. Secrets need to be guarded because they give a person insight into how to inflict harm. But I don't want to use anything Nicolas confides against him. That would be horrible. The worst kind of betrayal. No, I can't do that.

But the twelve Godmothers are counting on me. They've worked my entire life to bring down the Floren regime, citing its corruption and harms. They can't be wrong about this, not when they've spent so much time planning. I haven't found any of the horrors they've described to me over the years. No starving citizens, whispers about cruel torture, people being unjustly thrown in the dungeon or murdered. But Godmother Twelve is one of the Floren advisors. She must know what's wrong with the kingdom. I just haven't found it yet.

Should I push Nicolas away? I curl into a ball, wrapping my arms around my knees. I enjoy being around him. Matching wits has been the most fun I've had in years, topped only by our fight in the woods. The thought of getting into another sparring match sends my pulse thrumming with excitement. And while I don't want to look too closely at the way my heart flutters when he does something unexpectedly sweet, I can't ignore it either. No, I won't avoid him or try to put distance between us.

Knowing I'm intentionally defying the Godmothers sends twin bolts of fear and excitement through me. This is open defiance. There's no way my trips to the market and my friendship with the prince will go unnoticed by Godmother Twelve much longer. She may attribute it to my trying to learn about my enemy … but she might figure out the truth. I like Nicolas and his parents.

I'll have to be very, very careful.

When Nicolas barges into my room the next morning, I'm ready for him. He pauses in the doorway, disappointment etched on his face when he sees me on the settee wearing a loose jade day dress.

"Prince Nicolas, what an unexpected surprise." I give him a bright smile, putting the novel I was reading to the side.

"Lady Lynx, I thought you'd still be asleep after the late night."

And he thought he'd catch me abed. "I'm too excited. There's so much I want to see and learn about your kingdom."

"Unfortunately, we only have the morning. I need to meet with my father and Captain Rossi in the afternoon, although I'd much rather take my squire around town." He gives a dramatic sigh. "So, we need to make the most of it. Go get changed. I'll wait here."

"No need, I'm ready." I stand and smooth out a wrinkle on my full skirt.

"No, no, no. I can't take the princess out. I need my squire." Nicolas grabs his oversized hat off his head and waves it at me.

"I thought you might say that." I wink and drop the dress to the floor, revealing my tunic and trousers underneath.

He looks shocked for a moment, then bursts out laughing. "You're full of surprises, my little lynx." He tosses me the hat. "What do you want to do today?"

I jam it on my head, then link arms with him. "Anything outside the palace."

I'm in so much trouble.

16

I pull back one side of the dusty curtains. "Are you sure nobody will come in here?"

Nicolas coughs as he yanks back the other side, flooding the room with light. "Not for another two weeks, when they start preparing for the ball. We'll be fine." He busies himself opening the bags at his feet and laying the weapons out on the floor.

"And we're going back to the marketplace tomorrow, right?"

He chuckles. "We've gone every day for the past two weeks."

"But there's still so much to see. Like the apothecary shop and that odd music booth. Oh, and I saw a sweet maker we haven't visited yet."

"And you'll see it all, I promise. I'll take you every moment I can spare. But since it looks like it might rain, today's the perfect day for our rematch. Aren't you looking forward to sparring with me again?"

"Of course I am. I just want to make sure you'll take me

after I trounce you. You're probably a sore loser." I flip the end of my braid over my shoulder, then put my hands on my hips, surveying the empty ballroom.

The ceiling soars overhead, light sparkling off the chandeliers. A small dais for musicians sits on one side of the room, while the far end holds two thrones. The gilding on the walls glows in the sunlight, brightening the midnight-blue plaster. The light wood floor has an intricate knot pattern that's dizzying to look at across the expanse.

I shake my head. "We can't fight in here. I'd be afraid I'd scuff the paint or scratch the wood. Pick somewhere else."

"Don't you pay attention at the Cabriare balls?" He points to the wall to his left. "A lordling who shall remain nameless punched a hole there when he found out his mistress was seeing another man. And over there." He gestures to a spot on the floor. "A Council member smashed a tray of drinks because a trade deal fell through. This room is no stranger to violence."

"So, you're saying if I run a sword across the floor or stick a dagger into the wall, it's fine?"

He tosses me a knife from his crouched position. "Go ahead."

I finger the tip of the blade and walk a few steps closer to him. He rises, hands clasped behind his back.

I stop in front of him, pointing the dagger at his chest. "You're serious."

"Yes."

"And you won't stop me."

"Correct."

Keeping eye contact, I shift my grip on the blade. The knife drives into the wall an inch from his ear.

Nicolas doesn't even blink. "We should remember to grab that before we leave, otherwise the servants will get to speculating about what happened in here."

I grin. "Let them gossip. The palace could use a good mystery."

He holds my eyes a beat longer, then crouches again. "What's your weapon of choice, milady?"

So many good options. A variety of daggers, swords, small axes, staffs, plus a few I haven't seen before. "Sword."

He hands me a beauty: a long, light blade with a flower design worked into the hilt for grip. I test the balance, then swish it through the air, enjoying the *wish-wish* noise.

Nicolas picks out a slightly heavier blade and examines it, then switches to my sword's twin. "Should we pad the blades?"

"I usually fight with live steel."

"Me too."

My pulse thrums. While the lessons with Seven were punishing, I loved the freedom of fighting. And after our bout in the woods, I can't wait to see what will happen this time.

We walk into the middle of the floor and face each other, ready for our deadly dance. A beat. I swing my sword at his chest. He blocks me, pushing me back. One movement flows naturally into the next as we whirl and clash around the large room.

Fighting Nicolas is thrilling. Now that we're on level footing and equally armed, we're well matched, but different enough to keep throwing in unexpected combinations.

It's so much easier to fight in trousers. Freer movements and not worrying about a dress tangling my limbs lets me take larger steps and incorporate more leg attacks. The prince is caught off guard for the first few but quickly adapts to my style. Nicolas favors a traditional style but uses his strength to turn blocks into attacks and stay on the offensive.

The clash of steel echoes off the wall, accented by our grunts. The fight has lasted longer than any of my bouts with Seven. We're both tiring, but I'm not willing to concede, and I'd wager Nicolas feels the same.

There—an opening. I step in and press my sword against his stomach a second before his rests against the base of my neck.

We pant, locked in our killing positions, eyes glowing.

He says, "Draw?"

"Agreed." I wait until he moves his blade away, then step back, dropping the sword's tip to the floor.

He puts his weapon on the bag, then collapses on the ground in a sprawl. "Fewer banquets. More practice."

I lie on my stomach on the floor next to him, propping my head on my arms. "Are you as good with knives as you are with a sword?"

"You think I'm a good swordfighter?"

I groan and smack his shoulder. "Of course you are. Obviously not as good as me. But you deserve some praise for managing not to stab yourself."

"Where did you learn to fight like that?"

Dangerous territory. I should have expected this. "Same as you. Lessons all my life. It's important that I can defend myself. You never know what kind of trouble a princess can get into."

"Not all princesses, just you." He gives me a fond smile. "You're unique among the nobility. What can you do with a dagger?"

"Wouldn't you like to know."

"I hope someday you'll tell me."

"If you're lucky."

"What's Cabriare like?"

That's something I've wondered about myself. I pluck at the hem of my shirt. "What have you heard about it?"

"The normal dry details that don't amount to much. The same you'd heard about Floren, I'm sure. Flat geography. Gems, fish, and grain exports. That type of thing. But I want to know what it means to you."

Having never been to Cabriare, I can't say. But Nicolas deserves an answer—a *real* answer. So, I tell him about my home. About the way the moonlight plays across the fields. How the sunlight can soak right through your skin and fill you up. Endless hours of studying politics, geography, decorum. My collection of medicines and how I've developed my own blends. He tells me about visiting the marketplace over the years and sneaking into Council meetings when he was young just to fall asleep under the table. His worries about following in his parents' footsteps and ruling a kingdom. The projects he's worked on around the city and his plans to expand the water system, so people won't have to carry it long distances anymore. His dream to bring inventors from all over the world to Floren and make it the leader in innovation.

I teach Nicolas a push-sweep move, and he shows me how to break an opponent's grip when they have your arm locked behind your back. We spar, then talk, then spar, every match ending in a draw. We sneak to the kitchens and filch an armful of snacks, then run laughing back to the ballroom. It's easy to forget he's the Floren prince and I'm an imposter Cabriaren princess. We're simply two people getting to know each other.

He brushes a few crumbs off his trousers, then stands and offers me his hand. "Would you care to dance, milady?"

I laugh and swat at his hand. "Don't tease me. I'll make you pay for that in our next duel."

"No jest." He tugs me up and pulls me into his arms.

When I hesitate, he gently takes my hand in his and puts his other on the small of my back, his touch feather light. We begin to move around the dance floor.

Suddenly I'm all shaky knees and awkward limbs. It's not like I've never danced before. It was part of my lessons, along with languages, history, herbology, and a slew of other subjects. But this is different. My first real dance.

Nicolas glides smoothly across the wood, whereas I stumble like a newborn colt. But then I look at his gray eyes, and everything falls away. We twirl and spin around the room to a silent tune, just like the dancers on his machine.

The fading light in the ballroom finally calls an end to our day. The frivolity fades as we pack up the weapons and the remains of our snacks, but the lightness sticks with me as I float down the halls. Nicolas invites me to join the family for supper, but I beg off. As much as I like his parents, tonight I want to be alone with my thoughts.

It was a perfect day.

I wrap my arms around my middle. *Why does the thought make me sad?* Because I'll never have another one. But … I never thought I'd have this one. So, I'll treasure it and do my best to find the next one.

Mayhap that day is tomorrow.

17

I waltz to my rooms, humming a tune I overhead in the marketplace. The night lamps flicker in their niches as the few sleepy servants I pass give me amused looks. It's hard to keep the smile off my face as I remember the stories the king, queen, and Nicolas shared around the sitting room fire. I can't recall ever laughing that hard for so long. Just thinking about the horse loose in the banquet room sets me giggling as I push open my door.

"Gaia, you won't believe the story I heard."

Godmother Twelve's dry voice freezes me in place. "The servants aren't here."

She sips from a teacup, the liquid matching her dark eyes. Her thick, black hair is braided into its trademark crown around her head. At my dumbfounded stare, she nods to the chair across from her. "Sit."

I stumble across the room and drop into the seat, my hands and feet numb. "Godmother Twelve … I'm so happy to see you."

"Who is this Gaia?"

My forehead puckers. "One of the people you hired to pose as my staff."

"I've never heard of her. It seems you have a spy in your confidence. Oh, Aryanna, you're so trusting." She shakes her head. "I do hope you haven't told her too much. You know how you like to chat."

Rocks form in my gut. *She's a spy? I haven't told Gaia anything dangerous, have I? Nothing that would endanger the Godmothers' plans? Surely, I wouldn't be that reckless.*

She sets the teacup on the table and pulls out a folded paper stamped with the rose-and-thorn insignia of the Godmothers. "I've been getting disturbing reports about you."

I squirm in my chair, pressing my hands against the seat.

"Disappearing from your rooms. Trips to the marketplace. Spending time with the royal family."

"The king and queen invited me to take meals with them. I thought it would be suspicious to turn them down, since I'm supposed to be a visiting princess getting to know Nicola—the prince. I didn't see the harm in it."

Godmother Twelve sighs and pinches the top of her nose. "It's really my fault. I should have known this would be too much for you to take on, especially after Vivia fell ill. I thought I could trust you to manage on your own. Obviously, I was wrong." She looks up. "But no more. I'll be taking a more active role. You can still be useful to me. You just need more guidance and oversight."

I slide my feet under the chair. "I was trying to confirm what you've told me about Floren. Everyone here is so happy. I thought if I could find evidence …"

Her eyebrows shoot up. "You believe they'll casually mention they've been executing peasants and smuggling weapons to our enemies over dessert? These are conniving, manipulative people who have played the political game for years. You think you can trust a single word they say? Oh, Aryanna, my dear child."

When put like that, it sounds terribly stupid.

"We'll just have to manage the mess you've made the best we can. Don't change your behavior now, otherwise they might get suspicious. Continue to be friendly to the royal family and whoever this Gaia is, but don't tell them anything. If Vivia doesn't recover, I'll give you instructions when it's time to act." She slips the paper into her dress and stands. "I trust I won't be getting any more reports about you."

I stare at the carpet, the woven colors blurring together.

"Remember, no sacrifice is too great. The Godmothers will succeed at all costs."

The sharp snap of the door closing echoes around the room.

The royal family must be laughing themselves silly every night at how they're tricking the clay-brained little princess. Of course I can't find any evidence of their wrongdoing; they're around me every moment I'm not in my rooms. That's why Nicolas is spending so much time with me. *Keep her amused, flirt a little. Make her feel special. Take her places to keep her busy. She's too dimwitted to figure anything out.* I can see it now—I've made it so easy for them. Gaia is in on it too, since Godmother Twelve doesn't know her from her time in the Floren palace or as one of the people she hired for my entourage. Everyone around me is lying to me, and I've let them.

No wonder Godmother Twelve doesn't trust me.

And worst of all, I have to continue to smile and laugh

with them, knowing what a fool I've been.

How can I face them now that I know the truth?

18

The pattering of the rain outside plays on my nerves. I press my head against the window, staring at the streaks on the glass. My stomach writhes, trying to escape my body. After the conversation with Godmother Twelve last night, I'm not sure what to do. I don't want to face anybody today. Having to play nice while they're lying to my face might kill me. Or I might kill them. *I can't stay here.*

Impatient to be gone, I stick my head into the hall and pull a passing maid into the room to lace me into a pink day dress. Then I tie my hair back with a blue ribbon and grab the first cloak at hand.

I leave the wing and make my way to the palace's main hall. Servants going about their normal duties offer me nods and smiles, a few stopping to ask if I need assistance. I indulge in a few minutes of admiring the carvings and decorations. Remembering how I thought everything looked gaudy makes me cringe. It's really beautiful; I don't know how I could have been blind to it before. But I don't dare linger too long. If Godmother Twelve should catch me out here alone …

I pick a passage at random and start walking. Each room is a new treasure: parlors, music rooms, smaller libraries, dining rooms, and some rooms I have no idea what their purpose is beyond taking up space and being gorgeous.

According to the maps I studied at the villa, I'm at the east end of the palace near the laundries, butteries, distillery, and other assorted rooms that make life in the castle pleasant. The hallway splits at the end, one side leading to the smaller kitchen, while the other goes to the laundry and sewing areas. The faded tapestry at the intersection would be unremarkable except for being slightly askew on the wall. A closer inspection reveals the edge is caught in a small door tucked behind the wall hanging. *This wasn't on any of my maps.*

Intrigued, I open it to discover a black hallway. No lamps lit or even resting in the niches along the wall. A quick backtrack to one of the parlors yields a small hand lamp. I hesitate a moment, then step through and close the door behind me, checking that the tapestry isn't caught this time.

The hallway is dusty around the edges, but in the middle, the grime is scuffed or missing. *It would take more than one or two people to make those tracks.* Curiosity moves me along the passage at a quick clip, looking for evidence of where the people went.

There are only a few doorways along the walls. A peek inside reveals bare rooms with thick dust laying undisturbed. The passage turns and dead ends into a blank wall. The footsteps clearly lead here, but there's nowhere to go. *Unless … a secret passage?*

A thrill races through me. I was always searching for

secret passageways in the villa. Sadly, I never found anything there, but here's a chance to fulfill a childhood dream.

Unlike the rest of the palace with its plastered walls, the passage is a mix of bare stone in gray, black, and marbled. I hold the lamp close to the surface, studying the stones for any incongruities. Pressing on the raised portions of the wall yields nothing.

Hmm … Godmother Twelve once said the best place to hide something may be in plain sight, but it should be something a person can never find by chance.

A person could always stumble into a wall, but they could never pull it out by accident.

I dig my nails into one of the marbled stones overhead and tug.

The wall swings open.

A real secret passageway! I clamp my hand over my mouth to muffle the squeal as I jump up and down—then curse as hot lamp oil spills on my hand. Sucking on the burn, I inch around the door.

Another empty storage room. Refusing to be put off, I repeat my search of the stones inside the room. Any likely-looking spot within reaching distance gets tugged and pushed.

Nothing happens.

Disappointment threatens, but I focus on the accomplishment instead. Knowing about a secret room is always useful, and it's obviously important, since there's so many recent footsteps. There's something more going on here, and I've found the first piece to a puzzle. Mayhap there's more clues in the rest of the palace.

As I walk back toward the exit, I almost miss the small

doorway swinging open, flooding the passage with light. I freeze, then dive at the nearest door, shoving it open with my shoulder and slamming it closed behind me. I blow out the lamp and press my eye to the crack around the door.

"I don't know about this." Nicolas's voice carries down the hallway.

"We've already come this far. If we stop now, it'll be for nothing."

That hard voice belongs to Lia. I've never seen her inside the palace before, and nobody's mentioned her. Now that I think of it, I haven't met any of his friends except her.

"It's getting dangerous. I think some of the Council members suspect something."

My ears perk up. *This is the evidence I've been looking for.* The pang in my chest surprises me. *This is what I want, isn't it?*

"We're careful. If they're suspicious, it's because they're frightened old chickens with nothing better to do than to fret over every coin in their bulging purses."

Nicolas chuckles as they come into view. He's wearing an odd outfit. Shabby. Even the clothing the stable boys wear to muck out stalls is better than what he's currently dressed in. Lia matches him in tattered trousers and a long tunic, her red hair tucked under a shapeless hat. *What are they up to?*

They pause in front of my door, Nicolas with his back to me as Lia faces him.

He runs a hand through his dark hair, then gestures at the floor of the passageway. "All I'm saying is we need to cover our tracks better. If they find out, you know what'll happen."

"Don't worry about me. You just make sure you keep that royal neck of yours intact."

"Why, Lia, I'd almost think you care."

"I can take care of myself. But if you get caught, this whole thing has been for naught. Watch yourself. And don't let anything slip to your princess."

"Aryanna wouldn't turn us in."

The confidence in his voice warms my insides—until I remember he's a liar. But why lie to Lia about me? No, it's more trickery. He doesn't want her to worry. It's about comforting her, not defending me.

Lia pokes him in the chest. "Nicolas, don't you dare."

"You're wrong about her. But I won't say anything."

She puts her hands on her hips.

He raises his hands. "Fine, fine. She won't hear this from me. At least, not until she needs to."

Lia steps back, her mouth dropping open. "No. You can't possibly be thinking about it."

The prince clasps his hands behind his back. "I don't know what you're talking about." His tone is all innocence.

"You're actually considering courting her. The girl would've gutted you in the forest if I wasn't there to stop her. She's violent. And ruthless. You saw the way she handled that knife. It's not normal for a princess."

He grins. "Isn't it wonderful?"

Oh! I look at Nicolas with new eyes. I know we both enjoy bantering and bickering, but I thought it was all play. *Does it mean something more to him?* I press my hand to my lips, my skin flushing. *No, I need to stop this. He's a liar and a rogue. I can't trust him or anything he says.*

Lia glares at him, then stalks out of sight, muttering under her breath. Nicolas follows, whistling a jaunty tune that abruptly cuts off after a few bars.

I strain to hear anything else, but there's only silence.

After counting to one hundred, I open the door and stick my head out. Empty. They've disappeared into the hidden room, but why?

I want to go after them, but instead my sensible feet carry me to the small door and then into one of the fancy rooms, where I drop down on a couch and wrap my arms around a cushion.

Lia and Nicolas are up to something. It must be something big if they're concerned about the Council. But he's the prince. What could he possibly be doing that they need to worry about? Royalty is a law unto themselves.

My thoughts swing back to the Godmothers. Is whatever Nicolas and Lia are doing part of why the royal family needs to be overthrown? Godmother Twelve is on the Council. If she's discovered what they're up to, then mayhap the Godmothers' reasons for removing the king and queen are sound.

How can I discover what Nicolas is hiding, and if it involves his parents? What is it? I turn scenario after scenario over in my head, trying to find an answer, but I keep coming up with more questions than answers.

"Aryanna?"

I shoot up at Nicolas's voice and curse myself for sitting in plain view of the hallway when they had to return this way.

The important thing to do is to remember he's a liar. I can't trust anything he says. Even when he was talking to Lia about me and saying those nice things, it's only because he's manipulating her too. *Ugh, why didn't I at least close the door so they wouldn't see me and I could avoid this entire conversation? Burning fool!*

"Hello." I give him a chipper smile. "I was exploring the

palace since there's nothing on my schedule today and thought I would rest for a few minutes. Isn't this room lovely? All the rooms are lovely, actually. And it's so big. I could explore for days and days and not find everything. Not that there's anything I need to find."

He tilts his head to the side. "Are you feeling well?"

"Yes, quite!" I wince at the high pitch of my voice. "How are you?"

"I'm well." He glances at the dusty hem of my dress, then over his shoulder toward the small door. "What are you doing here?"

"I told you, I was exploring."

"And you just happened to come this way?" His eyes narrow.

I narrow mine right back at him. "Yes. What are you doing here?"

"Oh, some business." He makes a vague gesture.

"With livestock?" I look pointedly at his ragged clothing. It's hard to be sure with the dark material, but the bottom of his pants looks wet.

He watches me for another heartbeat, then his jovial mask falls into place. "Ruling a kingdom is dirty business. We save the silk for special events. Allow me to escort you back to your rooms, milady. I'd hate for you to get lost."

"No, thank you. I'm going to keep looking around. You never know what you'll find behind a door." I'm dangerously close to revealing what I know, but I don't care.

A glint sparks in Nicolas's eyes. "I can't risk you disappearing on me."

After all his teasing and torments, it's time to show him not all my skills are with a blade. I rise from the couch and sashay toward him, keeping my eyes locked on his. "Is it so dangerous within the palace?"

He swallows hard. "Very."

I stop inches away and look up at him through my lashes. "It's always better to have someone watching your back in such a perilous situation." A thrill runs through me. I'm playing with fire. "Do you have someone to watch yours?"

His eyes darken.

Lia stomps into the doorway. "He does." The redhead looks ready to breathe fire as she glares at Nicolas.

This keeps getting better and better. "Is that true?" I purr, running my finger down his arm.

Watching Lia's face set into stone is almost as good as teasing Nicolas. It's fun to deliberately flirt with a gorgeous guy. More fun than I thought. I'm alive in a way I rarely am outside of a fight.

Nicolas clears his throat, then tears his eyes away from mine. Disappointed, I drop my hand, ignoring the smirk on Lia's face.

She says, "We need to go."

He grimaces as he bows to me. "I'm afraid our tour will have to wait until another day. But please … be careful."

"I'm used to watching my own back. Enjoy your day."

"Aryanna—"

"Nicolas, we'll be late." Lia tugs on his sleeve.

With a last look at me, he follows Lia in the direction of the main hall.

I go back to the couch, refusing to give Lia the satisfaction of watching them walk off together. It's flattering to know I had an effect on him, but I don't let it go to my head—at least, not too much. He went with Lia, after all. He's probably not used to such brazen flirting. *Imagine if he had acted that forward with me?* I gulp. Now that I've opened this door, he might take advantage. I hope it wasn't a big mistake.

No, I can handle Nicolas. If he flirts with me, I'll give it right back to him and then some. A bubble of mirth rises in my chest as I imagine all the fun I'll have the next time we cross blades.

The bubbles fall flat. He's my enemy. How many times do I need to tell myself that before it sinks in? I'm doing half his work for him. No wonder Godmother Twelve is so disappointed in me.

It's my fault for not staying away from him after I arrived, like Godmother Twelve instructed. To be forced to continue this farce of a friendship while plotting his downfall is torture, but the punishment fits the crime. I need to keep my mind—and my heart—on my mission.

I mentally kick myself; I should have followed them. Another failure. But no, Lia will be keeping an eye out for me, even if Nicolas isn't.

Nicolas. I can't get him out of my mind. How he didn't deny Lia's words. The way his face lit up. I shake my head as his laughter fills my mind.

He only affects me this much because I haven't had a lot of experience around men. The Godmothers almost always hired women at the villa. Only a few males appeared over the years, and they disappeared quicker than the female servants. He's a novelty.

It's better not to think about why it's his face that caught my attention and not any of the other men at the palace or marketplace. I can tell myself it's because he's the one I'm supposed to be concentrating on for my mission, but a little voice in the back of my head whispers that's not the only reason. I tell it to be quiet. He's treacherous. No matter how honest and kind he seems, he can't be believed. I've already discovered one of his secrets with the hidden room, and that's proof enough not to trust him.

I wander around the palace the rest of the day, but the novelty is gone. After the supper hour passes and I'm sure Gaia will be gone, I take a circuitous route back to my rooms. I feel better able to handle Gaia and Nicolas now that I've had the day to think things through. It'll be hard to keep up the friendly appearance while maintaining my emotional distance, but it must be done. If I need a break, I can always slip away and explore.

Where there's one secret passage, there's bound to be more.

19

Gaia must sense my mood the next morning. Despite my attempts to appear cheerful and friendly, she's subdued. She delivers Vivia's daily health update, then gets straight to work. There's no singing as she straightens up the already tidy room. When there's a knock on the door, we both breathe a silent sigh of relief at the interruption.

The maid with the gray-streaked curls, Carmella, bustles in, followed by three footmen each carrying a large box. She and Gaia direct the men where to deposit their bundles before ushering them out.

Gaia claps her hands together. "Where did all this come from?"

"The prince." Carmella looks at where I'm hovering in the bedroom entrance, then whispers loud enough for me to overhear, "He picked everything out especially. Wrote a note to go with it too. Fussed over it for an hour, otherwise we would have been here right after breakfast."

"What does it say?"

"He didn't let any of us read it. Sealed it with wax

before I could catch a glimpse. But the way he blushed, it was the sweetest thing. You can see how much it meant to him." Her dimples are on full display.

I take a step inside the pale-green sitting room, my body drawn forward unwillingly. *It's a show for the servants. He doesn't actually care for me. It must be one of his games ... isn't it?*

Gaia walks around the large boxes. "I've never heard of the prince doing anything like this before. I wonder what got into his head." She winks at me.

"It's nothing, I'm sure." My fingers itch to open the packages. *I should send them back. Make him think twice about lying to me. But ... mayhap I should take a look first. I need to keep up the pretense that I like the prince. Ignoring his gift would be rude.*

I tear into the first box. The bundle of branches wrapped with a red ribbon makes me burst into laughter. *Our first meeting in the woods.* Gaia and Carmella gather behind me to look into the box, their faces reflecting their befuddlement at my delighted response to the odd present.

As I lift the lid to the second box, the sweet scent hits me: oranges. The box is filled to the brim with oranges. Nestled in the middle of the fruit is a small pot I know will contain tiny purple berries. *My first purchase in the marketplace; he remembered.*

The maid makes an appreciative noise. "At least that one's practical."

Gaia hums happily as I turn to the third box, excited to see what it holds. My fingers twist at the twine, tangling it in my eagerness. I yank off the lid and find ... *a jar filled with water and blue glass pebbles?*

She asks, "What does this one mean?"

"I—I don't know."

Carmella hands me a sealed note. "Mayhap this will help."

I break the wax, then smooth the parchment, squinting to read Nicolas's terrible handwriting:

> *The Lady Lynx has battled the woods and negotiated the market, but can she navigate the tides?*
>
> *Join me for our next adventure at half past the noon hour.*
>
> *Please come.*
>
> *The Red Bandit*

Gaia passes the note to her friend. "Not very helpful."

Carmella says, "What's all this nonsense about a red bandit and a lynx? I guess you'll find out what he wants this afternoon."

"Perhaps." I break off a piece of wax, rubbing it between my fingers.

The two women exchange a long look.

Carmella collects the twine. "I'll be off then. Good day, Princess. Gaia."

Gaia waits until the door closes to come over to me. "Aryanna?"

I burst out, "Why did he do this? Everything was fine. I knew what I had to do. Why is he making everything hard?"

She guides me to the couch, rubbing a hand in small circles across my back. "He wants to show you that he likes you."

"I know!" My voice cracks. "He shouldn't have done it. Why couldn't he have sent flowers, or jewelry, or a poem he copied from a book? This …" I wave my hand helplessly at the boxes.

"They all mean something to you? Something personal?"

"Yes." I long to pour the whole story out, tell Gaia the meaning behind each present. But I can't. She's the enemy too.

I pull a pillow into my arms and move away from her, wedging myself in the corner of the couch. Gaia folds her hands, watching me with a sorrowful expression. She mutters something under her breath, a glint of anger in her eyes.

"What did you say?"

"Sorry, sweetling. A bad memory overtook me for a moment." She reaches toward me, dropping her hand when I flinch. "Won't you please tell me why you're so distressed? I thought you liked the prince. Did he do something?"

"No. Yes. No. I don't know." The words fight to come out, but Godmother Twelve's warnings ring in my ears. "I just—I don't understand what he wants."

Her kind eyes watch me, encouraging me to continue without pressuring me.

My resolve crumbles under her understanding gaze. "He seems nice. But I've heard ... rumors. And I don't want to believe them, but what if they're right and I'm wrong? What if he isn't what he seems?"

I cringe at my own hypocrisy. *I'm passing judgment on him?* The person pretending to be Cabriaren princess and planning to overthrow his family's rule. If he's as bad as the Godmothers say, then we deserve each other. And if he's not, then I don't deserve his affection.

Gaia says, "Do you want to tell me about it?"

I bite my lip. *Yes—but I can't.* I shake my head.

"Would you like my advice then?"

"Please." Anything to help sort out this mess.

She stares at her hands, seeming to gather her thoughts, then looks up. "I don't know what you've heard or who told you. You need to judge whether they are a trustworthy source, or if they may have ulterior motives for what they said."

The Godmothers are trustworthy. I've staked my life and the lives of everyone in Floren on that. They've raised me, educated me.

But I can't reconcile the king and queen with the monsters the Godmothers described. How could they be killing people who whisper against them, and starving children, and selling citizens into slavery? Evil wears many faces, but there's not a wisp of malevolence around them. But the Godmothers have told me they're the villains. If I can't believe the family that raised me, then who?

Gaia says, "As for Nicolas, he's a good lad. He doesn't give his affection or attention away easily. Once he considers you a friend, you have his loyalty and support for life. Everyone likes him, but I think few know him. You see through the humor he uses to get people to underestimate him. He has a sharp mind, and he'll do what's right, even if it isn't easy."

She laughs. "Don't go believing he's perfect. He has as many faults as the next one. But if I had a daughter, I would be pleased if he courted her."

Her words only twist me up more. "But how do I know who to trust? How can I tell who's lying?"

"Only you can decide that. When I have to choose, I pay attention to what my head says, then my heart. Usually, they're telling me the same thing if I listen closely enough." She pats my hand. "I know how hard this is. When I was young, I was involved with a group of people who I thought were working to make the world a better place. But after a time, their words and their actions didn't sit right with me. It broke my heart to leave them."

I swallow hard. "Was it awful?"

"The hardest thing I'd ever done. They were my family. Closer, even. I didn't know how I would survive without them. But every day, things got a little easier, and I found a new family I could love. My only regret—well, let's just say I'm still working on fixing it." She gives me a fond smile. "So. Are you going to find out what adventure the prince has in store for you?"

I squeeze the pillow against my chest, pondering her words. At the villa, we were so isolated. Coming here has opened my eyes to a much bigger world than I ever imagined. My heart has been warning me that something isn't right, but I can't pinpoint what it is. Is it just the strangeness of this place playing tricks on me? That I'm homesick? Nervous? My head won't make sense of things. The Godmothers are my family. To disbelieve them is a betrayal of monumental proportions. But when the stakes are this high, is blind loyalty the answer?

Nothing has to be decided today. I can go with Nicolas, keeping an open mind, and see what happens. As Gaia said, I should listen to my head *and* my heart.

I clasp her hands. "What does one wear to an adventure?"

I peek around the corner, spotting Nicolas pacing in front of the palace's front doors. He stops to say something to Carmella, then resumes pacing.

Going with him doesn't mean anything. I'm keeping an open mind. I'll decide what I believe for myself. It's perfectly fine to spend time with him. Alone. It won't be the first time we've been alone together. Just because he sent me some thoughtful presents and invited me instead of dragging me off doesn't make this different from any other day out together. This is the same as going to the marketplace. Another fun day with Nicolas, nothing more.

Who am I fooling? Wetting my lips, I press a hand to my chest to calm my racing heart. *It's Nicolas. There's no need to be nervous. Go.* I step around the corner.

"Aryanna!" Nicolas dashes over to me, his face splitting into a huge grin. "You came."

The flutter in my stomach intensifies. "How could I possibly resist such an intriguing invitation? You're driving me mad with curiosity."

"Then my plan worked. I knew a lynx's curiosity would overcome any doubts."

His excitement at my appearance belies that confidence, but it's flattering he was worried. Carmella gives me a small wave behind the prince's back before slipping away.

Nicolas tucks my hand into the crook of his arm as he leads me outside. "I'd have preferred to go on horseback, but we'll be more comfortable with the carriage. I'd hate for you to freeze before we get there."

"Where are we going? Your gift was very mysterious."

"It's a surprise."

Nicolas lifts me into the carriage, his hands lingering on mine for a moment. Heat rushes into my cheeks, and I slip down the bench, breaking our contact. *Don't rush into anything.*

He climbs in, then looks out the door. "Where's Carmella? She's our chaperone for the afternoon."

"I believe she's abandoned us."

"Oh." He looks perplexed. "I'll go get her. Or there must be someone else who can come with us."

Laughing, I put a hand on his arm to stop him. "We'll be fine, don't bother anyone. They have plenty to do without us interrupting their day."

"But—but—we need a chaperone." He runs his hand through his dark hair, leaving it adorably rumpled. "It's not proper to go without one."

"Now you're worried about propriety? What about those times you've burst into my rooms, or the days in the marketplace?"

"This is different!"

"Why?"

"It just is." Nicolas mutters to himself. "Lia might be in

the kitchen."

My eyebrows shoot up. "You want *Lia* to be our chaperone?"

"No, you're right. Terrible idea." He sighs. "I just want to do things properly this time."

His earnestness touches me, and I soften. "Nicolas, this is fine. I'm fine. Nobody is going to care that we don't have a chaperone. Besides, it's not like I can't defend myself."

He looks torn—then relaxes. "You're right." He shoots back up. "I forgot something."

Before I can stop him, he leaps out and trots to the stables. I shake my head. *Something funny has gotten into him.*

The prince returns with an oversized basket. "Here." He hands me the soft gray blanket folded on top, then uses a rag to lift out a small ceramic pot, which he places near my feet. The temperature inside the carriage jumps up as heat pours out of the container.

I reach my hands toward the small pot. "That's wonderful, thank you."

He beams, then knocks on the roof of the carriage. The vehicle takes off with a lurch, the wheels clacking along the stone courtyard.

"Now will you tell me where we're going?"

"Patience, Princess. You'll find out soon."

He keeps me laughing as we travel out of town and down the road in the opposite direction from when I first came to Floren. The countryside changes from tightly clustered homes to rocky hills. Nicolas points out different landmarks and holdings, seemingly delighted by my interest in his kingdom.

The climate gradually takes on a heavier feeling, an odd

tangy scent hanging in the air. After we pass a large
monolith, Nicolas tugs me to the window and I gasp.

We've been transported to a magical water realm. The
huge white cliffs create a small pocket valley at the base,
filled with mist from the dozen waterfalls flowing down the
rocks, sprays dancing through the sunlight and throwing
rainbows into the sky. The falls each pour into a small basin
nestled at their bases, creating a series of terraced pools
filled with clear blue-green water. Steam rises from the
surface into the winter air. Men in black robes work inside a
small open structure tucked against one of the rock walls. A
small beach lines the nearest side of the pools, while lush
greenery rings the space, making it an oasis.

"It's beautiful."

"Do you like it?"

"I love it." I can't tear my eyes away from the view. To
think such a magical place is so close to the palace. "The
world is truly a wondrous place."

"Then what are you waiting for?" He opens the door
with a flourish, the balmy air rushing inside.

I tumble out and race to the water's edge. The steam is
warm enough to make my cheeks flush. Crouching down, I
run my fingertip along the surface. It's like touching
sunshine. The bottom of the pool is a mosaic of speckled
white stones scattered on pink-and-yellow sand, creating
fantastical patterns in lazy waves and swirls. The clear water
makes it seem like the pool is only a few inches deep, when
really it's at least fifteen feet down.

I plunge my hands in, marveling at the heat. "What
makes it stay warm?"

"They're thermal springs. The theory is they're heated
by lava underground before coming to the surface, hence the

odd smell. We have pockets of them here and there, but this is my favorite. The water is supposed to have healing properties."

I can see why. I'm happier and more relaxed simply by being here. The roaring falls play in the background, drowning out the rest of the world. Black-and-pink butterflies flitter around us, then disappear into the greenery. Fronds the size of carriage wheels mix with dark-green, waxy leaves longer than my legs. A flock of bright-blue and orange birds watches us curiously from the bushes. They cheep inquiries at us, fluttering their tiny wings, their eyes bright.

We linger by the water, sitting on the edge of the pool and dangling our feet in as we talk. Nicolas tells me about his travels, and I share some of the places I want to visit. He's surprised I've never been to anywhere but Floren, but never makes me feel less for not having the experience he does. Instead, he asks me about my interests and what attracts me to the places I hope to see.

"The coast is supposed to be riddled with caves where kingdoms hid their warships. I'd dearly love to find a forgotten ship."

He tugs a strand of my hair. "You'd make an excellent captain. I volunteer to be your first mate when you start terrorizing the high seas."

"Commission accepted. Lia can be the weapons master, since she's so fond of stabbing things."

"You'd let Lia play on your ship?"

"Of course, she's your friend." My grin turns sly. "Plus, as her captain, I could boss her around."

He bursts into laughter. "She'd hate that."

"And I'd love every minute." The smile slips from my

face, and I stare sightlessly into the water. *Should I ask? I need to know who I can trust.* "What were you and Lia doing that day in the palace?"

He's silent long enough that I peek at him from the corner of my eye. He drums his hand on his knee. "Aryanna, there's nothing more I want to do than tell you. But it's not my secret to share. It would put other people at risk."

Not the whole truth, not a lie. What am I supposed to do with that?

He touches my hand. "I know it's not the answer you wanted, but it's the one I can give. Can you understand that?"

It hurts, but I can. It isn't fair to ask about someone else's secrets, and I wouldn't trust him if he divulged them. He's been more honest with me than I've been with him. He still believes I'm Aryanna, the Cabriaren princess. He doesn't know anything about my life or why the Godmothers brought me to the palace. That I was plotting against him and his parents. What I should be asking is if he'll ever forgive me when he finds out.

"Nicolas …"

A man in black robes approaches. "Highness, it's time."

"Wonderful." Nicolas pulls me to my feet. "Wait until you see this."

I breathe a sigh of relief. I don't know what I was going to say, but it wouldn't have ended well.

He pulls me along the edge of the pools as the man trails behind us.

"Don't I need my slippers?"

"No, no, we're not going far. But I forget my manners! I should offer to carry you."

"If you even try, I'll—"

My words cut off as he sweeps me into his arms and continues clambering over the rocks. I cling to his neck, gritting my teeth.

"Oof, you're heavy."

"Then put me down, you oaf."

"What kind of gallant prince would I be if I forced you to damage your delicate feet on these sharp rocks? Nay, I will suffer for my lady. Just tell Gaia you don't need so many layers next time. You're so swaddled, I'm afraid I might drop you."

"Don't you dare," I screech as he wobbles, his grin wide.

"You wouldn't feel a thing with all the clothing you have on. You'd bounce across the rocks. And we're here."

He successfully distracted me from realizing we've reached a large pool at the base of a rock wall. Tied up at the edge are a dozen strange flat-bottomed boats that seat three or four people.

The man steps into one of the boats, then holds out a hand. "My lady."

At Nicolas's encouraging look, I take the man's hand and board the craft. I move to the front as the prince climbs into the middle. The man uses a long stick to propel the boat across the pool to a small crack at the base of the rock. It's low enough that I duck as we go through the cramped opening, running my hand against the stone overhead. *Wet?*

Nicolas whispers, "We can only access this cave when the water goes down. There's theories about tides and water flow causing the drop, but nobody is certain why the levels change."

Curiosity piqued, I fold my arms on the bow and let my eyes adjust to the growing darkness. We glide through the small tunnel, water dripping around us. The air is perfectly still, broken only by the sounds of our breathing.

The rock overhead disappears, and the boat drifts out into a large cave. My heart skips a beat, and I reach back to take Nicolas's hand. This really is an enchanted fairyland; no place on Earth could be this beautiful without the heavens reaching down and touching it. The water glows with a vibrant blue light, dimly illuminating the space. It's like sitting inside a sapphire. Above us, the walls sparkle like the night sky, reflected in the water below, wrapping us in stars. My fears are soothed away by the timeless peace that exists here. The boat has carried us through the veils, and we're sailing in the midnight sky. We're adrift in the universe, the world one of the shining spots around us.

It's impossible to say how long we've been here. Each heartbeat is a lifetime, every breath an eternity. Our lives before the cave are a dim memory that fades further and further away. The moment is captured, stretching out to the horizon, enduring forever.

My contemplation of our infinite paradise is interrupted by a fast-moving spot of orange in the water. "Look!" *It must be a fairy.* I dive to the side, trying to catch another glimpse of the creature.

The frail boat rocks, water sloshing over the edge as I dip dangerously close to the surface. The movement throws me off balance and I flail. "Ahhhhh!" Water rushes at me. I close my eyes, bracing for the dunking I'm about to receive.

A sudden jerk, and I'm flying backward through the air before landing face down on top of Nicolas, his face a breath from mine, my body pressed against his. I gulp, my mind a fog. Everything happened so quickly, it's hard to bring reality into focus. I blink, trying to clear the daydream, but all I see are the stars and him. *Nicolas.* My hands grip his shoulders as I try to breathe.

"Are you all right?" His brow creases, and he runs his hands down my arms. "Anything broken or bruised? Aryanna?"

Our eyes meet. His breath catches, and his hands tighten on my arms. My pulse races.

Are his lips are soft as they look?

The guide clears his throat. "Apologies, but we must return. The cave entrance will be submerged soon."

I scramble up, my face burning.

Nicolas says, "Of course, thank you."

The man poles the boat back. I dart looks at Nicolas, blushing and ducking my head whenever I catch him doing the same at me. As the boat emerges into the sunlight, I lift my face, expecting the spell to break. But the dream has followed me into the real world, softening its sharp edges, making it warm and welcoming in a way it's never been before.

Back on shore, we thank the man and gather our abandoned belongings. The carriage ride home is filled with unspoken words. Energy crackles between us.

He walks me to my room, lingering outside the door. "I'm glad you came."

"I should be thanking you. It was wonderful. I can't believe somewhere like that exists." I smooth my skirt, then look up at him through my lashes. "Are we going to the marketplace tomorrow?"

"I have to meet with the Linarian delegation in the morning. But I'm free in the afternoon if you're willing to wait."

"Mayhap I will, mayhap I won't."

Nicolas lingers over my hand, then reluctantly pulls

away. "Until tomorrow."

21

Tension crackles in the palace air. Nicolas is uncharacteristically grim as he explains how the negotiations fell apart with Linaria and the delegation stormed out of the city. The king and queen are gathering the Council to discuss what it means and what they should do next.

The prince strides through the palace hallways, his face set in harsh lines. "It was clear they weren't open to negotiations from the start. It was probably a ruse to give them time to scout the city and the palace."

"Evaluate your defenses without arousing suspicion," I agree. "Strategic, but obvious. They don't seem concerned about hiding their intentions."

"They're willing to make bold moves with minimal risk. I'm willing to wager coin those delegates were low-ranking spies. People who wouldn't be able to tell you about Linaria's plans if they were captured."

"No, they'll be people with military training who can assess Floren's strengths and weaknesses. There was no fear of capture. They know you'd never offend Linaria by arresting their delegates.”

“They’re right. We’d never risk war without evidence of treason. And arresting them with anything less than absolute proof would be war.” He rubs his forehead.

I pull him to a stop. “This is a game. Moves and countermoves. The important thing now is to keep a clear head and look at the big picture.”

He gives me a wry grin, then gently tugs a strand of my hair. “That’s what my father always says.”

I stare into his gray eyes. “He’s a wise man. You should listen to him.”

“Very.” He steps closer … then sighs. “They’re waiting for us.”

“Right.” I take a deep breath. “Right.” I push past him and march down the hallway.

“You’re going the wrong way.”

I spin around, my hands on my hips. “Am I actually going the wrong way, or do you just want to escort me?”

“Both.”

He holds out his arm, and I take it with a laugh.

The Council room reminds me of the room in the villa where the Godmothers hold their meetings. It’s a plain chamber with a large round table in the middle. Floren’s crest—a white lily on a red background—is barely visible in the center of the table beneath the maps and documents. Three chairs sit on one wall next to a small sideboard with carafes, cups, and papers. I attract a few curious looks, others more disapproving. Everyone appears to be a Council member except for myself. No servants so the conversations will be confidential and minimize leaks.

I whisper to Nicolas, “Mayhap I should leave.” Tensions are high enough without having a foreigner eavesdrop on their meeting.

He waves his hand dismissively. "Ignore Lord Franco and Lady Ginerva. Your attendance has already been approved."

I'll never understand Florens. So trusting with strangers.

Most of the members are already seated. Lady Rosamund and Lady Elisabetta were at the garden party. Lord Farland is easily identified as the portly gentleman with a bulbous nose. Lady Valentina is the taller woman, and Lady Ginevra has a small mole on her cheek. The other three Council members I haven't met before, but identify them from the descriptions from the Godmothers: Lady Eleonora and Lords Abromo and Franco.

Godmother Twelve is in attendance. She pays me no mind as I linger along the back wall, so I follow her lead. I'm still stunned she's part of the Council. She would know the inner workings of the palace, the politics, everything. All my doubts and questions come rushing back. *Why does she need me? There's no reason she couldn't have taken me into her confidence earlier. Why hasn't she visited me again? Do I want her to?* I shove the thoughts to the side. *Now's not the time.*

Nicolas directs me to a chair at the edge of the room, then takes a seat at the table next to his mother.

The king stands and calls their attention. "As you're aware, the Linaria delegation left this morning." He summarizes the items they were discussing and the delegation's abrupt halt to the negotiations. "We want to avoid warfare if possible. We all remember the devastation caused by the Ghibelline war. Floren is strong, but another armed conflict would make us an easy target for our enemies."

The Godmothers never told me about a Ghibelline war.
It sounds like it was relatively recent, within a generation or
two. I'll ask Nicolas or Gaia about it later. It's harmless
enough that my question won't raise any suspicion.

The king continues, "We must proceed carefully, while
preparing for the worst. I open the discussion." He returns to
his seat.

The Council members start with why the negotiations
fell apart. As expected from politicians, the discussion
quickly disintegrates into blaming people for the failure. The
king gently steers them back to what preparations Floren
needs to take and how to best defuse the situation.

Lady Valentina pounds her fist on the table. "Their rude
behavior cannot go unanswered. This is an offense against
Floren. We should demand reparations from Linaria."

Lord Farland nods, hands resting on his protruding
middle. "It's unforgivable. They may as well as sent a
declaration of war."

The bushy-haired Lord Franco squints and holds up his
hands. "I don't find Linaria's behavior so unforgivable that
we should risk the kingdom."

The arguments continue. The king makes occasional
comments to keep the Councilors on topic while the queen,
Nicolas, and Godmother Twelve are silent observers. When
the other members appear to run out of steam, the queen
speaks. "Lady Serafina, you've had the closest dealings with
Linaria. Please, offer your counsel."

Godmother Twelve steeples her fingers. "The head of
the delegation, Rantidio, is a fool. The king of Linaria
selected him for this venture precisely because it should have
been simple. But Rantidio is desperate to display his

importance, so he puts on a show for his entourage. The king will be angry with him and eager to make amends. I propose I visit Linaria to demonstrate we hold no grudge against them for this man's actions. I'm sure they'll welcome our message of peace and continue the negotiations."

The king and queen nod, but Nicolas shakes his head.

"With all due respect to your insights, I believe this is more than a peacock attempting to fan his feathers. Captain Rossi reports members of the delegation were observing the army maneuvers outside the city, wandering into the guards' barracks, and touring the outer walls."

Lady Elisabetta presses a hand to her throat. "Did they explain their actions?"

"Paltry excuses of being lost or wanting to see the city. They were bolder than they should have been because they know we'd never risk offending Linaria by arresting their delegates."

Godmother Twelve says, "An interesting conclusion."

To anyone else it would sound like a neutral observation, but I shiver at the subtext in those words. When I heard that tone at the villa, it was followed by an order to report to Godmother Seven for another training session—and the corresponding set of bruises.

Nicolas says, "It makes sense with today's events."

Lord Franco furrows his bushy gray eyebrows. "I agree. If the Linarians are being this audacious, it cannot bode well. The prince's instincts should be heeded, lest we pay for it in blood."

"I can't claim all the credit. Princess Aryanna and I came to the conclusions together."

As heads swivel my direction, I bow my head to acknowledge Nicolas's compliment, keeping my face neutral. Godmother Twelve's eyes linger on me a moment longer than the rest, then she turns back to the prince.

"I would still counsel caution. Once the drums of war are sounded, they cannot be undone. I can visit Linaria and return in two weeks with my observations. We should be sure of the situation before we take any actions."

The king and queen look at each other, the silent conversation of people who know each other intimately flowing between them. The king rises, offering his hand to the queen.

"Thank you for your wise counsel, as always. Queen Renata and I will discuss this further and let you know what we decide."

Everyone stands and bows as the king and queen leave the room. The Council members group in twos and threes, discussing the situation in somber voices. Godmother Twelve remains in her seat, her amber eyes fixed on me. My stomach knots, and the hair on the back of my neck rises.

Nicolas comes over. "Shall we?"

I grip his arm tightly, putting him between me and the Godmother's gaze. "Yes, please."

22

Gaia pins the last braid into place. "You look lovely."

I can't disagree with her assessment. My black braids weave around a delicate silver-and-sapphire tiara, the gems perfectly highlighting my blue eyes. The heavy hairstyle forces me to keep my chin up, giving me a regal air. My dress is dazzling: a light silver-blue threaded with silver strands so it shimmers in the light, making me appear as though I'm glowing. I'm not sure the white fur wrap will ward off the chill, but it looks elegant with the dress. Thank the heavens she rejected the dainty slippers that matched the dress and found my white fur boots in the closet, otherwise I'd lose my toes to frostbite.

I pat one of the braids. "Gaia, you're a genius. But I can't help but feel silly going to this performance when there's so much tension about the Linarians. Surely there's a better use of our time than parading around town."

"That's precisely why you and Nicolas need to make this appearance. Everyone needs something to keep their minds off the threat of war, otherwise tensions will continue to rise.

There could be fights and mobs in the city. People could panic. A happy distraction is the perfect way to release the pressure."

Clever. The king and queen aren't misleading the people but giving them something else to focus their energy on. I'd never realized fairs and performances could serve a purpose beyond amusement. The threat from Linaria won't go away, but having a spectacle today will allow the people some breathing space to better manage their fears and worries.

My companion says, "Vivia is doing much better."

I almost ask her who she's talking about but manage to stop the words before they escape. *Godmother Eight.* I'd forgotten about her. My stomach sinks. "That's wonderful. Please pass along my wishes for her recovery." I clasp my hands in my lap, holding on tightly. "Do you … do you know if she'll return soon?"

Gaia shakes her head. "She isn't in any danger now, but they don't want to risk whatever she has spreading. The doctors are quite puzzled by her illness."

The bands around my chest loosen. "I hope they find out what caused it." I jump up, picking up my skirt. "It must be past time to meet Nicolas—er, the prince."

"Don't forget this." She hands me a bundle of white fur. Seeing my puzzlement, she demonstrates, tucking my hands into both ends so they're encased inside. There's a few small heated stones inside the material, warming my hands instantly to a delicious degree.

I give her a bright smile. "Thank you."

She pauses, her eyes filling with tears as she puts a hand against my cheek. "You're such a sweet girl. Your parents would be very proud of you."

I look down and smooth my hand across the fur to hide

my confusion. *Would they?* I know she's talking about the Cabriaren king and queen, but how would my real parents feel? The Godmothers told me my parents were completely dedicated to the Godmothers' cause, but would they support me being here in the palace and plotting against my hosts, who have been nothing but kind and welcoming?

I shake my head to chase the thoughts out. Right now, I need to meet Nicolas for our outing into the city. Sadly, I can't go as his squire this time. This is an official celebration for the Prince of Floren and the Princess of Cabriare.

Heads turn as I walk through the palace to the front entrance. My cheeks heat under the admiring gazes and I lift my chin a little higher. I quicken my steps as I imagine Nicolas's reaction to seeing me in this gorgeous outfit. My heart skips a beat when I catch sight of him waiting at the entrance with a small contingent of guards.

He's stunning. Nicolas's coat and cloak perfectly match my dress. A neat trick. I wonder how long ago that was arranged. He spots me and goes completely still, his face going slack.

My lips curl into a self-satisfied smile, and I drop into a deep curtsy. It's gratifying to know I have some sway on him. He always seems so confident, like he knows exactly where he belongs in the world and is happy to be there. Seeing him off balance once in a while makes him feel more like Nicolas and less like "the prince."

He's shaken out of his stupor by a man plucking at his sleeve, trying to get his attention. Nicolas gives me a wry grin. He's someone who doesn't take the pomp of royalty too seriously. Someone who laughs at life while making sure the people around him are cared for.

Someone I could easily fall for … have fallen for.

It hits me like a blow. The air rushes out of my lungs. *I love him.*

No—I must be mistaken. It's because I've been spending so much time around him. Yes, that's all it is. But a persistent voice in the back of my mind quietly insists I'm lying to myself.

Meeting Nicolas changed everything for me. He isn't the spoiled, boring prince I thought he would be. He's not even the arrogant bandit I met in the woods. He's sweet. Kind. Frustrating. Funny. Intelligent. Overconfident. Loyal. Proud. Thoughtful. There's a thousand words to describe Nicolas and none. He's simply Nicolas, and that's everything.

He showed me a different way to think about things just by being himself. That people should be treated with respect. That a kind word can make all the difference. That wanting to be happy isn't selfish.

There was no defense against it. It sneaked up on me without my ever suspecting it was coming. I can't pinpoint the moment it happened because it's hundreds of moments. Every laugh and smile and conversation piled on top of each other until here I am, standing in the palace entrance, feeling like the floor has disappeared from beneath my feet.

All these thoughts pass through my mind in the blink of an eye, but everything has changed. Colors are sharper, brighter. Noises louder. The cold bites my exposed skin with a new intensity.

Nicolas gestures for me to join him. I shuffle across the distance as my mind struggles to reconcile my new reality with the old.

"You're breathtaking. Truly a dream come to life." He offers his arm. "Ready for our debut?"

All I can do is stare dumbly at him.

"Aryanna?" He peers into my face. "Are you feeling well?"

I snap back to myself and give him what I hope is a brilliant smile. "I'm fine. Let's go perform for the people."

Lady Rosamund is waiting inside the carriage to act as our escort. She chatters at us, seemingly content with our nods and noncommittal noises as she talks about the parties and performances this week.

I can't stop staring at Nicolas, no matter how many times I order myself to turn away. He gives me a puzzled smile, but otherwise seems undisturbed by my daft behavior. *How can he just sit there? Doesn't he know the world has turned upside down?*

The prince of Floren. Even if I were a normal girl, he'd be out of my reach. But this … this is a disaster of monumental proportions. I'm here to dethrone his parents and turn the country he loves over to the Godmothers. It's not exactly something he'll forgive and forget when he finds out. *Nicolas, I know I was responsible for upending your entire life and getting you thrown out of the kingdom, but I love you. Would you like to have dinner with me?* Not the best way to start a relationship.

Everywhere I look are problems. Assuming the heavens grant me a miracle and Nicolas forgives me for my past, the Godmothers are expecting me to fulfill my role. They won't look kindly on my falling in love with their sworn enemy. Godmother Twelve is already disappointed with my performance, and this won't help my case. And I still don't know who to trust. When the time comes to act, I'll have to pick a side.

What am I going to do?

Too soon, we alight from the carriage in front of a large

building. The people gathered outside wave and cheer, tossing flowers at our feet. I'm acutely aware of Nicolas at my side, as charming and handsome as ever as he greets them, many by name. Every nerve in my body is attuned to his movements. Every brush of his hand against mine sends my pulse racing.

Inside the building is worse. The nobles descend on us like a flock of locusts to say hello, request favors, or just bask as perceived friends of the prince and princess. I keep the smile pasted on my face as our circle of space grows smaller and smaller until I'm pressed against the prince's side, my skin on fire.

After I'm sure I'll explode if I have to spend one more minute there, Nicolas extracts us from the press with a smile, and we escape to a balcony. I finally have a few seconds to catch my breath and calm my racing pulse as I take in the theater.

Our seats give us an unspoiled view of the stage below and give everyone a perfect view of us. The upper nobility fill the seats behind us, chatting excitedly about the upcoming events.

We wave to the crowd filling the lower area. Most appear to be merchants and other citizens. There are a few of the lesser nobles mixed in, easily picked out by the sour expressions on their faces.

A nearby guard hands Nicolas a bouquet of white lilies and a wrapped bundle.

He passes them to me. "Gifts to remember the occasion."

Oh! I clutch them to my chest, my eyes wide. "I didn't get you anything."

"Your presence is gift enough."

His teasing drains the tension from me. *This is Nicolas.* He doesn't know my feelings have changed. As far as he's concerned, we're putting on a show, playing the parts of young royalty falling in love.

I hold the flowers up, inhaling their perfume. "You're too magnanimous, Prince Nicolas, as your presence is gift enough to me. Nay, I'm in your debt."

"Then I look forward to collecting." He takes my hand and kisses my palm as the nobles around us sigh.

The heat from his lips lingers on my skin. I keep my gaze down as I hand the flowers to the guard next to me, then unwrap the bundle to find a wooden case. Nicolas' eyes light up as I lift the lid and gasp in delight. Nestled in the velvet is a stunning dagger that could only have come from the swarthy stall owner. The silver hilt has a large sapphire worked into the pommel, while the grip is an overlapping wave design that brings the ocean to mind. The blade is simplicity itself, but even more lovely for the craft work. Next to the blade sits a thin thigh sheath.

I snap the lid shut, hoping the nobles didn't see. *Why would Nicolas give me a weapon?* I know why he would give *me* a dagger, but not the Cabriaren princess. For a real princess, this would be an entirely inappropriate gift. But I can't help but be pleased. The knife is perfect: a playful reminder of our first meeting, practical, and beautiful.

I run my hand down the case. "It's lovely."

"The moment I saw it, I knew it was meant for you." He interlaces our fingers together and rests them on the chair arm.

My insides melt as tears prick my eyes. He can't know what torture it is knowing he doesn't mean the feelings behind the actions and words. Though he's fond of me, mayhap even likes me, it's a drop in the ocean compared to what I feel for him. But just because it's an act for him doesn't mean I can't enjoy the ruse. *I'm going to make this a day to remember.*

I relax back into my chair, prepared to relish every moment.

The entertainment is ideal for distraction: games. They start by having tumblers and jugglers flood the stage, warming up the crowd. I laugh and cheer along with the rest of the people, pointing out my favorites to Nicolas and admiring his. He's as caught up in the fun as I am. Fire breathers run out, shooting flames between the performers. We shriek and gasp as a blaze appears to engulf a tumbler who then bursts through the wall of fire unharmed, to deafening cheers.

After the troupe leave the stage, the wrestling starts. The first match features a large muscular man with a long beard, facing off against a shorter bald man. The bearded man waves and taunts the crowd, while the bald man shakes out his arms and legs, not glancing at the people calling for his attention.

Nicolas laughs. "This should be over quickly. That little man doesn't stand a chance."

"Don't underestimate him. He's shorter, yes, but solid. He'll take down his opponent."

"A wager, then."

"What shall we bet?"

He taps a finger to his chin. "Coins?"

"No, it has to be meaningful."

His eyes glint with mischief. "If I win, my squire will accompany me to Cova de Perla. There's some caves there I'd like to explore. Mayhap find a lost ship. You have to climb down the cliff wall using a rope. Definitely too dangerous for a lady."

My pulse quickens, and I'm so happy I could burst. *He remembered!* I yearn to explore those caves … but not enough to let him win. What can I ask for in return? "Supper. The two of us. Outside the palace." Not as exciting, but something I desperately want.

He pretends to think it over, then holds out his hand, palm up. "Agreed."

I press my palm to his, sealing our bet.

As the two men on stage circle each other, I scoot forward in my seat, gripping the railing. Nicolas presses in beside me.

The bearded man makes the first move, darting forward. My champion darts to the side, making the larger man chase him. *Smart.* First he'll tire out his opponent, then go on the offensive.

Nicolas bellows, "After him! Destroy him!"

Not to be outdone, I yell, "Keep him off balance!"

The excitement in Nicolas's face matches my own. We turn back to the fight, cheering on our chosen competitors.

The bearded man stumbles. The bald man makes his move, hooking a foot around his leg and grabbing his head. The larger man tumbles to the ground with a resounding boom. My favorite jumps on him and gets him in a headlock.

The crowd roars as the giant thrashes on the ground, the smaller man clinging to him, wrapped around his body with arms and legs. The thrashing gets weaker … then the large man taps his opponent in surrender.

Nicolas groans as I pound on the railing.

"Impossible. How did you know?"

"Never underestimate a person because of their size—or

their gender." I lean back in my seat, smiling triumphantly.

He waves his arms. "It was a fluke. I demand a rematch."

I heave a dramatic sigh, secretly enjoying his antics. "Fine. I can't have you pouting and grumbling that I won by chance. But this time, if I win, you take your squire to those caves." I hold out my hand.

He presses his palm to mine. "And if I win, you have to be nice to Lia."

I yank my hand away. "No bet."

"Too late, the bet is made." He grabs my hand and presses a kiss to the palm again.

My anger melts away, but I keep the frown on my face. "Why should I be kind to her when she's as like to stab me as not?"

"She's not that bad once you get past the remarks and hostility." He leans closer, lowering his voice. "Please? She's a friend. I would like it if you were friends with her too. She doesn't have many."

I mutter, "What a surprise." I brace myself for the pang of jealousy, but it doesn't come. He cares about his friend. And I'm sure it would make his life easier if we stopped snarling at each other every time we're in the same room.

"I'll do my best to—" I look out of the corner of my eyes at the nobles eagerly eavesdropping on our every word— "not make any *cutting* remarks. But if she draws blood first, the truce is over. Assuming you win. Which you won't."

He rubs his hands together. "Bring out the competitors."

23

Nicolas buries his head in his arms and moans into the rough wooden table. "Six matches. Six!"

I pat his shoulder. "There, there. You came really close on that last one. Have another drink." I signal the server with the same motion he used earlier.

The tavern seems wonderfully downtrodden and coarse. We're seated at a tiny table crowded into the dark corner, our knees bumping into each other each time one of us shifts. The air is hazy with smoke. A chill seeps in through the cracked window, but a roaring fire across the room keeps the room a tolerable temperature. The men at the long table wave their wooden mugs around, sloshing beer onto the floor. Two women in veils whisper together by the door, three men and a woman in furs wager on a tile game at another table. Most of the other seats have solo occupants nursing drinks and staring moodily into their cups or enjoying a bowl of stew.

Nicolas raises his head high enough to glare at me. "Your patronizing is worse than your gloating."

I beam at him. "I know."

The server bustles over with two tankards beading with moisture. She plonks them on the table, the foam sliding down the sides. "Anything else, dearie?"

Nicolas says, "Two meals. And my dignity, if you can find it."

"I'll check in the kitchen."

I giggle as she flounces away. "I hope she does. You need something new to wager next time."

He shakes his head. "I've learned my lesson. I'm never betting against you again."

"Where's the fun in that?"

"A man needs to salvage some pride." He takes a long pull on his drink. "I thought you'd pick somewhere a little more elegant for your supper."

"No, this is perfect. Look at all the interesting people. Imagine where they came from or where they're going."

He surveys the room, his brow wrinkled. "They don't seem that fascinating."

"Because you're not seeing what's underneath. Like those people in the furs. They're traders from the mountains. I'd love to sit with them and hear their stories."

"Could you leave Cabriare one day?"

Easily, since I've never been there. "Of course. I've known my entire life I won't stay there. But I don't mind. The world is full of amazing places."

Nicolas props his head on his fist, his eyes full of curiosity. "Like what?"

"Like the blue cavern you showed me." My mind flashes back to the books I've spent days poring over, soaking in every description. "And the sea. How it stretches out into the horizon, hiding a world of wonders under its surface. I've read about waves that reach higher than a castle's tower."

"But Cabriare is a seaside kingdom. Surely you're used to it by now."

Too late, I see my mistake. "You can never be bored by the sea. Besides, I want to see a wild sea. Cabriare's is so sheltered." *Time to change the subject.* "Would you ever leave Floren?"

"I did for two seasons. There was an inventor who invited me to study at his workshop in Germania. We worked on everything from large machines that bring water down from the mountains to villages, to delicate craft works that please and delight, and everything else I could have imagined. It was one of the best experiences of my life, but it also taught me how much I love Floren. I can't imagine calling anywhere else home. There's so much I need to do to keep it safe."

"Floren isn't safe?" I shudder. *He's right.* The Godmothers have a plan to overtake Floren, and they can't be the only ones. *What allies are they working with? Should I warn him?* My loyalties are so divided; there's no clear path. I want to confide in Nicolas, but knowing he's plotting something with Lia keeps my mouth shut. Despite my love for him, there's still mysteries surrounding the prince. The people of Floren need protection too.

He leans back in his chair and crosses his arms. "What kingdom is truly secure? There's always an enemy looking for a weakness. Someone scheming, believing they can do better than you. But tonight isn't about politics."

I let him lead me away from the topic, wanting to keep from spoiling our evening. "You're right. Tonight is about me gloating. And you wallowing." I tap my tankard to his.

I study him as he drinks. "Why were you in the woods

that day?"

He coughs. "Wh-what?"

"The day we met. Why were you there?"

The tips of his ears redden. "No reason."

"Nicolas ..."

He pulls the tankard closer, wrapping both hands around it. "I wanted to meet you."

I make a dismissive noise.

"No, really. My mother had spoken about your mother over the years, and she was so excited about your visit. I admit now, I was a bit jealous. And curious. So, I went out, hoping to catch a glimpse of you before you arrived. See how you acted before you put your guard up." His smile turns from sheepish to teasing. "Imagine my surprise when the Cabriare princess attacked me."

I flick my foam at him. "If you weren't acting like a bandit, I wouldn't have attacked you. Skulking around, wearing a mask. It's no wonder I thought you were up to no good."

"I don't think my being a bandit is the reason you came after me."

"No, but it was a good excuse if the Godm—someone asked me why I did it."

He bursts out laughing, causing heads to swivel our direction. "Only you would think that. Any other princess— any other person—would've run back to the group for help. But not you. You decide to take on an armed vigilante with a stick."

"It was a really big stick. Besides, I can take care of myself."

"Obviously. But it doesn't mean you can't have someone watching your back."

My mind flashes to his friend. "Like Lia?"

"You're not still worried about her, are you?"

"Not in the way you're thinking." I push my drink between my hands, trying to put my feelings into words. "I like that you care about her, even if I don't know why. And she'll skewer anybody who looks at you funny, so I guess she's not completely detestable. I just … I don't understand why you're friends. You two seem so different."

He mulls over my comments. I scrunch my toes and try to keep my hands still. I'm happy he's trying to give me a thoughtful response, even if it's driving me crazy with impatience.

"I can see why it would look strange from the outside. We both bonded over our love of Floren. She's even more protective than I am, if you can believe that. That's why she's so prickly with you. She worries you'll put Cabriare's interests ahead of ours."

"That's the only reason she's doesn't like me?" I arch my eyebrow.

He laughs and holds up his hands. "You're right, she's not really given to liking people at the best of times. But if you earn her loyalty, you'll have it forever."

"I'll settle for not having to keep my knife ready around her."

"That's one of the things I like about you. You don't give trust easily either, but you don't push people away like she does."

I fold my arms on the table and lean forward. "What else do you like about me?" It's brazen, but I don't care. I want to know.

"You don't back down from a fight. You're funny. You gloat when you win." He leans closer, his lips a breath away from mine. "And you know how to handle a dagger."

I could kiss him. Just lean forward and brush my lips against his. Nobody else would ever have to know. We're invisible here, just another couple sharing a meal at the inn.

The server drops two chipped wooden bowls on the table with a clatter. We jump apart.

She says, "There you go, loves. Anything else?"

Nicolas clears his throat. "No, thank you."

"If you change yer minds, wave." She leaves to check on another table.

My mouth waters at the delicious aroma. Parsnips and other vegetables in brown gravy with chunks of meat. I grab the flat tin fork and dig in.

Nicolas looks dubiously at his bowl. "How does it taste?"

"Good," I grunt. "Try it."

Nicolas scoops up a bite of stew. He sniffs it. "What is it?"

"Does it matter?" I laugh as he wrinkles his nose. "Parsnips, turnips, mushrooms, carrots, meat." I take another bite, savoring the thick gravy.

He slowly lifts his fork. With a last grimace, he pops the chunk of turnip and meat into his mouth and chews slowly. "Not bad." He makes a face. "I'm not sure what the meat is, though."

"Meat is meat. Enjoy it."

"Rosa's spoiled me. She makes the most beautiful roast beef dish with gravy and tiny onions. Once you've tried it, you can never help but compare everything to it."

"I had no idea you're so picky. What do you eat when you're out campaigning with the troops?"

"We don't. The farthest the army moves is right outside

the city walls."

"It never travels?" I pause, my fork halfway to my mouth. "Don't you patrol the borders or do practice maneuvers in different terrains?"

He pushes a piece of turnip around the bowl. "Why are you so interested?"

"I'm not. But I find it curious that you aren't. For all your talk of protecting Floren, it sounds woefully unprepared for an attack."

"The borders are managed by the local towns. We provide money so they can hire guards and patrols. The city is the heart of the kingdom, so we make sure the standing army can defend it."

"But the city could be surrounded. They could cut off your supplies and wait you out."

"No, they can't." He winces. "But I'll talk to my father about it. There's nothing wrong with having some of our own people patrolling the borders." He jabs a parsnip with his fork.

He takes a lot of responsibility on himself. It would be easy for another prince to shrug off the concerns of ruling a country and leave it to his parents. "Do you ever want to run away? Give it up and leave all your duties behind?"

"For about two seconds … but I could never leave my city. There's so many things I want to do, so many ways we can help the people."

"They seem pretty happy already. What else can you do?" *Is this the rot I've been searching for?*

"The nobles and the ones we see in the marketplace, sure. But everyone should have an opportunity to build a good life." A shadow passes over his face. "Some people never have a chance. And that's not right."

Like Lia, I'd wager. "What's needed? Better orphanages?"

"That and so much more. Basic schooling for children. Reinforcing the buildings on the hillside. Finding a second water source for the city in case the current one goes dry. Improving drainage for the winter storms. Hospitals that help everyone, regardless of class. There are too many lives lost from simple injuries that go untreated, and disease is one of the greatest threats to the city. We can't stop it, but we can lessen the damage."

"You don't do anything by halves! That sounds like enough work for three lifetimes."

He runs a hand through his dark hair. "Right now, they're just ideas. There's so much that goes into implementing even one of them that it's overwhelming."

"But you don't have to do it alone. Isn't that what the Council is for?"

"They can't agree that the sky is blue. Getting them to approve anything takes a miracle. If I can get my parents behind the ideas, I have a chance, but they're so busy, I hate to burden them. Every time I want to bring up a project, something happens. Like this situation with the Linarians." He stares into his mug. "It's not their fault, but it makes me wonder if things will ever change."

I put my hand on his. "They will. Because people like you care and will do whatever they can to make it happen. Be patient. You can't build a city overnight. Little changes add up over time. Mayhap there's a smaller project we could work on to get things started."

"I'd like that." He gives me a tired smile. "I see how my parents get caught up dealing with politics and making bargains they don't want to, so that the kingdom survives, and I know someday that'll be me. It's not something I'm looking forward to."

My heart aches at the weight on his shoulders. "I can't promise that won't happen, because part of being in charge is making those decisions. But I do know when the time comes, you'll make the right ones. Because you'll always have the best interest of your people at heart."

He squeezes my hand, then sits back in his seat, seeming to withdraw into his thoughts.

We busy ourselves finishing the cooling stew. I try to recapture my earlier happiness, but the ease is gone. Nicolas makes a few attempts to keep his lighthearted act going, but after a few minutes, he lapses into silence and stares glumly at the table. He doesn't protest when I suggest we leave.

Back at the palace, we unsaddle the horses and turn them over to the stable hands.

He rubs the back of his neck. "I'm afraid I wasn't very good company tonight. Let me make it up to you."

I shake my head. "I don't expect you to put on a cheerful face every minute we're together. I'd rather we be honest with each other." And it's true. While the evening didn't turn out the way I anticipated, I wouldn't change a thing. I got another glimpse into what he hides from the rest of the world, and I'm grateful he felt comfortable enough to share that part of him with me.

"So would I. It's nice having someone to talk to about these things. Most people can't understand why I worry or care. But you do." Some of his lightheartedness returns as he dramatically places a hand over his heart. "But I insist on a do-over. I must repay my debts."

"I consider this wager paid in full. There are, however, five other wagers I plan to collect."

He offers me his arm. "I shall fulfill each and every obligation."

24

The marketplace seems emptier than in past visits. I look for my favorite arms dealer, but there's no sign of the swarthy man or the fluttering crimson streamers that mark his stall. Nicolas is busy bartering with a woman over a new tool that has him very excited, but I'd rather wander to see what new discoveries await.

The man at the nearby table demonstrates a tin machine with lots of levers. He throws around descriptions about tension and gear ratios as I debate buying it as a surprise for Nicolas. I can't follow the explanation of how it works, but it reminds me of Nicolas's enthusiastic description of how he built the delightful contraption for little Elena.

Someone bumps into me from behind. *My coins!* Nicolas warned me about pickpockets. I spin around, but the person has already melted into the crowd. My hand goes to the dagger strapped to my thigh, relief rushing through me when I find the hilt still there. I curse myself for being complacent as I dive into the throng after the thief.

The guttural tones of Ranuvia catch my ear. Two small,

dark men with closely cropped beards mutter to each other as they navigate through the marketplace. "*Sret yun ... ilker a ... en reti ...*"

It takes a moment to translate: tomorrow, queen, blade.

The hair on the back of my neck rises. *The queen is in danger.* But from the Ranuvians? It doesn't make sense.

I slip through the crowd, following the men at a discreet distance, thanking the heavens my squire outfit makes me less conspicuous. They don't seem to pay attention to anyone around them, overconfident in their foreignness to offer privacy.

The crowd thins as the men travel down a side street. At first look, their clothing appears modest, but the cut and materials hint at wealth. I slow my steps, creating a greater distance between us, but keeping my gait purposeful so as not to draw attention.

They disappear through a door. I walk past it and around the corner, then cling close to the wall as I round the back of the building. A narrow alley barely wide enough for me to squeeze through separates this group of buildings from the next.

"What are you doing?"

I swallow my shriek, spinning around to smack Nicolas on the shoulder. "Don't scare me!"

He rubs the spot with a wounded expression. "I wasn't trying to. But you ignored me when I called out to you. What are you doing here?"

I quickly fill him in on what I heard.

His playfulness drops away. "Ranuvia? Their delegation is coming tomorrow. They requested Mother be present for the negotiations."

"That's not unusual, given her history with them." When

he gives me a surprised look, I add, "The peace treaty between Ranuvia and Flaminia fifteen years ago. She presided over the negotiations. Let's find out what's going on before we do anything drastic." I gesture to the building they entered. "I'm going to take a look."

"You can't spy on them. What if you get caught?"

This is child's play. "I'll be fine. Stay here."

I slip away before he can stop me. The series of low windows covered in shutters offers the perfect cover while I peek inside. A large open space with some crates pushed against the wall. No sign of the men. My heart races—*I've missed them*—then I spot the stairway to a loft area tucked in one corner.

I hurry back to Nicolas and drag him around the corner, catching him up as we run to the front door. Dagger in hand, I push him behind me as I open the door. He gives me a bemused expression, then falls into step behind me, his knife at the ready.

The stairs haven't seen much use. I test each step before moving despite Nicolas's growing impatience. We can't give ourselves away to the men upstairs. We might not learn their plans for the queen—not to mention a prince and a princess caught spying on foreign delegates would be a political disaster.

The loft is divided into rooms, presenting a puzzle. Remembering the secret tunnel, I direct his attention to the floor where the dusty footprints lead to the far door.

Nicolas and I creep down the hallway until I can hear voices.

"… will she be there?"

I grip Nicolas's arm—*it's them!* I inch toward the door.

"The secretary confirmed it yesterday."

"We should wait until after—"

"We've already agreed. Giving her the crystal knife first can only help our negotiations. It shows we come in friendship and remember her assistance ending the war. This treaty will benefit both our kingdoms. Everything we do to show goodwill is only for the better."

My shoulders relax, and I let out a quiet breath. Nicolas raises his eyebrows; I shake my head and smile. He draws a hand down his face and gives me a relieved grin.

The voices fade as Nicolas and I slink back. I feel ridiculous for the unneeded drama, but I'm relieved there's no danger.

Before we reach the stairway, the door at the end opens.

No time. We can't be seen. I haul Nicolas through the closest door and shove it closed behind me. It's a storage closet, barely large enough to hold the two of us. I hold my breath as footsteps walk past our door. They pause at the top of the stairs. I slowly realize I'm pressed against Nicolas's chest, his arms wrapped around me. The two men exchange words, but I can't hear anything over the buzzing in my ears.

He runs a finger down my cheek, and my breath catches. His heart thunders under my hand. His gray eyes darken as they stare into mine, capturing me.

Nicolas. Somewhere at the back of my mind is a weak protest I should stop, but I ignore it. What's coming is as inevitable as the sun rising in the morning.

He tilts my chin up. I push up on my toes, pressing my lips to his.

Oh! It's the only coherent thought my mind forms before I'm lost. His lips are impossibly soft, his touch tender. The world disappears until there's only the two of us. I wrap my arms around his neck, and he pulls me closer, burying a hand in my hair. A fire starts in my belly and spreads through my body until I'm consumed in flames. Something inside me shifts, pulling my heart to his.

Slowly, slowly, the world comes back into focus. I reluctantly pull back, then steal another kiss before breaking apart. He looks at me, stunned, as we stand pressed together, breathing heavily.

Outside, footsteps retreat down the stairway. A few moments of silence, then a door closes.

His arms tighten. "Aryanna … my love." He bends down to kiss me again.

My body stiffens.

Aryanna.

But I'm not Aryanna, Princess of Cabriare. I'm an imposter sent to dethrone his family. I betrayed his trust before we even met. He can't love me—he doesn't even know me. He loves the idea of a rebellious princess who gets her hands dirty—a princess who doesn't really exist.

I have to tell him. But I can't. He'll hate me when he finds out the truth.

And I love him.

"We—we should go." I turn away as tears prick my eyes.

What have I done?

25

When we reach the market square, I make a vague excuse why I need to slip off. I can sense his reluctance to leave me, but I'm insistent, and we can't talk about what happened in the middle of the marketplace. Nicolas gives me a long look before turning away and stumbling to the stables.

Once he's lost in the crowd, I pull the oversized hat low over my eyes and wrap my arms around my chest, hurrying off in a random direction. I need time to gather my thoughts before returning to the palace. I don't slow down until I'm thoroughly lost in the city, taking arbitrary turns as I go.

I kissed him. What does it mean? How could I do that? We kissed! What is he thinking? What do I think? I've ruined everything. He kissed me. But what will happen now? What does he want from me? My thoughts chase after each other around my mind, swirling in a dizzying windstorm.

He'll know I'm an imposter soon enough. And when he finds out, he'll never forgive me. He'll be hurt. He doesn't deserve that. I'll never forgive myself. Why did I let my feelings get involved?

I can't pretend it didn't happen. It did! That kiss will be on my mind until the day I pass from this world and go into the next—and even then, I can't believe it will fade. No, pretending isn't an option. But as much as I can't ignore it, I also can't believe it solves anything.

There's no hope for us. My feet stumble and I lean against a wall, putting my hand against my aching heart. No matter what I decide, Nicolas and I can't be together. He's a prince, and I'm an orphan who conspired against him and his family. Even if he's willing to fight convention, it's political suicide. The Council would force him off the throne. Nicolas loves Floren. He belongs here; it would kill him to leave. *I can't do that to him.*

Telling Nicolas the truth about me will destroy me, but it might ease his pain in the long run. If he realizes I'm not who I say I am, he'll let me go. But would shattering his illusion be the right thing to do? It could make him bitter and angry. Prevent him from trusting the next woman who catches his eye. It might be better if I simply disappear or tell him a lie about why I have to leave.

My wanderings are interrupted by three men who see a lone traveler as easy pickings. Dispatching them is an interesting diversion, getting my mind off my predicament for a few minutes. But using the beautiful dagger Nicolas gifted me quickly brings my mind back to him.

Ignoring their groans, I wipe the blade off on one of my would-be assailant's cloaks then pick up their knives. I should go back to the palace, but I'm not ready to face him.

Everything has gotten so confusing since I came here. Before I met Nicolas, I knew exactly what I had to do. I had a purpose.

Now I'm lost. I can't betray him and his family … but I

can't turn my back on the Godmothers. They raised me. Took me in when nobody else would. And my parents—they died for the Godmothers' cause. I'm rejecting their legacy, everything they wanted for me.

Gaia said listen to my head and my heart, but they're both as tangled up as I am. I close my eyes and take a deep breath, digging my nails into my palms. It all comes down to one decision: do I tell Nicolas about the Godmothers' plot, or do I push aside my feelings for the prince and fulfill my destiny?

Nicolas or the Godmothers—who can I trust? There's only one way to find out.

Urgency snaps at my heels as I sprint to the top of the hill.

The secret door swings open. I step inside, holding the lamp high.

What did Nicolas and Lia do in here? It's possible they wanted to have a private conversation without eavesdroppers, but there are far simpler ways to do that. And it wouldn't explain their ragged clothes.

Where there's one secret passage ...

It takes over two hours to locate the stone that triggers the trap door. I've covered the room three times before I finally spring the mechanism. I almost cheer as the black stone in the far corner lifts and slides to the side. A narrow ladder leads down into darkness.

At the bottom, my boots splash into a shallow stream. *That explains why their clothing was wet.* The tunnel dead ends a few paces behind the ladder, the water coming from a narrow gap too small for a rat to wiggle into.

The other way is more promising, leading off in the direction of the outer palace wall. The ceiling is low enough that I have to duck my head and hunch over. It's hard to tell how long things take down here, but I'd estimate I've traveled outside the palace grounds before the tunnel branches.

The water flows off to the left. I take the right side, leaving a trail of wet footprints on the dry stones. It abruptly opens up into a large square room filled with barrels and crates.

What are they up to?

I find a pry bar among the containers and start exploring. Barrels of apples. Crates of blankets. Guard uniforms. Swords. Hardtack. Grain.

My stomach knots. It looks like supplies for an army.

I replace everything, then explore the other tunnel. The water deepens to knee level, and I thank the heavens I'm wearing my squire outfit instead of a dress. The air fills with a sour stench, making me wrinkle my nose. As the chamber-pot smell grows stronger, I put my sleeve across my face and take shallow breaths out of my mouth. I'm about to turn around when a large iron gate covering the end of the tunnel comes into sight. Fresh scrapes on the stones confirm it's moved recently. The area behind the grate is undoubtedly the city's sewer system.

I hurry back to the storeroom then through the palace to my rooms, trying to avoid as many people as possible. After a quick wash and change into a fresh tunic and trousers, I search out a maid to request a tray be brought to my room. I'd rather fetch it myself from the kitchen, but I want to avoid any more wagging tongues, and I'm not in the mood to be cheerful.

My feet wear a path in the decorative carpet of my sitting room as I think through my findings. The crates and other containers weren't dusty or showing signs of settling, so they weren't collected over time. Nicolas and Lia must be responsible for them. But they can't be acting alone; there would be an uproar if all the supplies there had gone missing. Are the king and queen involved, or do they have other conspirators?

It doesn't matter. The Godmothers are right. There's something going on that stinks around here, and it isn't that sewer. My hands clench into fists and grind my teeth when I consider how I've been taken in by all of them. Nicolas especially. I've been an even bigger fool than I feared. To think that I—no, it doesn't matter. I know better now.

I need to keep my heart out of it. From now on, I'll be using my head to make my decisions.

My heart gives a sad pang. I tell it to be quiet. My mind's made up, and there's no changing it.

The important thing is to discover what they're doing with those supplies. The answer I keep coming back to is supplying a secret army, but to what purpose? Where is the army located? Who is a part of it? My pacing continues, increasing with speed as my agitation grows.

The door opens and I stumble to a stop.

Godmother Eight walks in.

26

"Godmother Eight—" I slap my hands over my mouth.

"It's well we're alone, else you would have just lost us everything." Vivia curls her lip. "Is this how you've been conducting yourself? Running around the palace in this … costume?"

"Yes. I mean, no. I was, um, in the city. I had to wear a disguise." I cringe at the flimsy explanation. "I'm glad to see you've recovered." My eyes creep up to the white streak in her black hair. *I swear it's grown wider.*

"Your concern for me is overwhelming." She leans on a thick, knotted cane to walk over to the couch, settling heavily on the cushions. "Godmother Twelve has told me of your antics. We have a lot of work ahead of us to repair the damage."

The anger radiating off her sends me shuffling back a step.

"Go to sleep. Tomorrow, I'll remind you how to behave."

My feet automatically carry me toward the bedroom

before my mind catches up. *The supplies in the tunnel.* "Godmother, I—"

"What now, you silly girl?" She mops her head with a handkerchief and mutters, "Serafina had better be right. This is more trouble than it's worth."

There's no reason to hold back, but I can't force the words out. *The Godmothers already have their plans in place. Telling them about the secret room won't change anything.* It's cold comfort knowing I'm keeping Nicolas's secret while still working against him.

"Well?"

"My weapons," I blurt out. "I haven't been able to find them."

Her eyes slide away from me. "That's no concern of yours. When the time comes, we'll make sure you're taken care of."

A shiver runs up my spine.

Godmother Eight spends the next day drilling me on behavior and decorum. The three lectures on proper attire and five lectures on ladylike behavior are the highlights of the morning. Servants occasionally make an appearance with trays and to clean, their cheerful demeanor evaporating as the Godmother harangues them from the moment they enter the suite until they flee at the first opportunity. Gaia is conspicuous in her absence.

After the supper invitation from the queen arrives, my stomach flips from butterflies to nausea every few seconds. I'm excited to see Nicolas and dreading it. I owe him an apology for leaving him in the marketplace, but I don't know if I'll be able to keep from shouting at him now that I'm aware of his plans. Only knowing my betrayal is greater lets me keep the tears at bay.

Vivia sends a terrified maid into my closet in search of a dining outfit, then continues her lecture. "You will not speak unless spoken to. Cover your mouth when you laugh or smile. I swear, if you show one tooth—no!"

The maid freezes by the closet door, the freckles standing out in her pale face. She clutches a light-blue gown with a ruffled skirt to her chest.

Vivia charges at the girl, her cane waving in the air. "Are you trying to make her look like a harlot? Demure. Modest. Hurry!"

The maid disappears into the closet with a terrified "Eep!"

The Godmother turns back to me, smoothing her hair back. "Be polite, but not memorable."

I chant along with her in my head. *Sweet, but not simpering. Intelligent, but not witty.* In other words, be boring. Don't be myself. What would Nicolas think of me if we'd never had our fight in the woods? Would I have acted the idiotic little princess, or would the monotony have bored me to tears until I acted out? Would he have bothered to say more than two words to me if I had played my role to perfection?

My head reminds me I don't really know him, that he's not the person I thought he was. My heart shouts back that there's an explanation, that I need to give him a chance to tell me what's going on. That those afternoons of stories and fights and laughs are the real Nicolas, and this villainous Nicolas is the lie.

What a pretty tale I tell myself. *He's as bad as the Godmothers say. Worse. He deserves what's coming to him.* My heart's protests weaken as I repeat his guilt over and over.

"… and above all, don't be too forward with the prince."

Heat rushes to my cheeks as I remember our kiss. *Too late.*

She hits my arm with her cane hard enough to bruise. "Don't bite your lip, Aryanna. How you managed to forget all your training, I'll never understand."

The maid creeps out of the closet, holding a brown velvet dress in front of her like a shield. The plain dress has a high collar, with sleeves that lace to the wrist, and a long skirt that will brush the floor even at my height.

"Finally, something not completely inappropriate." She snatches the garment out of the maid's hands. "What are you waiting for? Find the shoes, you incompetent girl!"

"Shouldn't you—" I snap my mouth shut. The maid overheard all of Vivia's instructions. If word got back to the king and queen, they may suspect something is wrong. But I don't want to get the poor girl in trouble, and I don't trust Eight to leave the maid unharmed if I point her out as a potential liability.

"What, Aryanna? Don't stand there flapping like a fish."

"I—I—there's a matching set of gloves too."

She heaves an overwrought sigh. "Have you forgotten everything? Gloves are never worn for supper."

"Oh, of course. I'm sorry."

I pull the dress over my head, then grip the bed's bannister as the Godmother laces the back up. My nails dig into the wood, my mouth pinched shut as she yanks the strings tight, her knee pressing into the small of my back.

My breaths are shallow as she ties the lacings off. I focus on moving my lungs as she works on the sleeves, then goes back and loosens them slightly when I can't bend my elbows. I resemble an overstuffed straw doll about to burst at its seams. Between bouts of harassing the maid, she loops my hair into a tight twist and pins it within an inch of its life.

The yellow dining room, normally so cheery, looks sickly in the candlelight. The king, queen, and prince are seated when we arrive. King Luka is oddly sitting at the head of the table, while the queen occupies the chair next to Nicolas.

Queen Renata and King Luka. The loss hits me in a black wave. It doesn't matter that everything they've done has been an elaborate act to keep me from knowing their true nature. For a time, they felt like my family, and now they're lost to me forever. The injury is real, even if they aren't.

Nicolas. Seeing him again, knowing the depths of his betrayal, almost kills me. His beloved, hateful face. Those expressive gray eyes full of lies. Only pride keeps me from crumpling to the floor. I hate him almost as much as I hate myself. Even if he had some small smattering of feelings for me, he'll move past them soon enough. But I shudder at the pain I'll cause him when I take Floren away from him. I'm committed to helping the Godmothers take back their rightful places, but I'll never forgive myself for hurting him.

Vivia says, "Forgive our tardiness, Your Majesties."

Queen Renata says, "No forgiveness needed, Lady Vivia. We're delighted at your recovery. Please, sit."

A horror grows inside me as the Godmother takes a chair. *Gaia never joined us. Should I have invited her?* I didn't mean to slight her. She's another who lied to me, but I didn't know that at the time. I would hate to think I mistreated someone. My regrets are piling up this week.

I take the seat next to Vivia and across from Nicolas. He's studiously examining the cuff of his sleeve, blatantly ignoring me. I drop my eyes to my plate and keep them fixed there as the courses are served.

The queen gives me up for a lost cause after a few attempts to draw me into the conversation. Vivia is clearly pleased with my brief responses. I mentally shake my head. How can she believe this is an effective strategy to get the royal family to like me? I'm as dull as an unsharpened sword. But I can't muster the energy to care. My thoughts drag, and it takes a tremendous act of will to raise my fork for each bite.

Nicolas's jovial mask is back in place, but there's an edge to his words. I wish there was a way to signal him I don't regret our kiss. That I'm sorry for getting scared and confused. My despair of loving him, knowing he's not who I thought he was. The fury at how he's lied to me since the moment we met. The frustration crawling under my skin that I have to be the tool of his downfall when all I want to do is fall into his arms and kiss him again.

But I don't dare bat an eyelash under the Godmother's watchful eyes.

Supper grinds on around me, the conversation stilted and pained despite the king and queen's best efforts.

The beet I'm slowly crushing with my fork gets a brief respite when the king's comment catches my attention.

"Linaria sent a message. They're planning to attend the ball next week. An interesting turn of events, given the way they left the negotiations."

The queen raises an eyebrow. "Very interesting." A series of silent messages passes between them.

My troubled gaze meets Nicolas's across the table. My heart leaps—then plummets when he turns away. I drop my eyes back to my plate and return to destroying the beet.

Why would Linaria come back? Their very public and dramatic exit signaled a desire to cut ties with Floren. Are they going to conduct another scouting mission?

Nicolas says, "We should have someone mind them while they're here."

Vivia says, "To what purpose?"

There's a long pause at the table. The king and queen have bland expressions, but there's a tightness around the queen's eyes.

Nicolas's scowl melts into a charming smile. "To ensure their comfort. We usually assign several palace servants to assist our guests by fetching trays, running errands, and finding their way around the palace. You have several attendants assigned to your quarters."

"Ah, yes. They've been very … helpful."

After an uncomfortable silence, the queen turns the conversation to preparations for the upcoming ball. She chatters lightly, the king and prince throwing in an occasional comment. A vague memory of Gaia mentioning the ball surfaces in my mind, but I hadn't realized it would be so soon.

There's a chance for all kinds of mischief at an event like that. That many people together makes it easy for an enemy to sneak in and out without being noted. I listen, hoping to hear about the security precautions, telling myself it's for the Godmothers' sakes, but they frustratingly keep the conversation on court gossip and entertainment.

The interminable meal finally ends. Nicolas leaves without glancing my direction. The queen looks like she wants to say something to me, but instead takes the king's arm and bids us a good evening. All I want to do is collapse into bed and forget the whole terrible day. My lead-filled feet drag on the carpet, the effort to lift them too much for my exhausted body.

The Godmother detours when I turn toward my rooms, pulling me to one of the lesser-used areas of the palace. "Your evening isn't over yet."

I'm unceremoniously shoved inside a room, the door banging shut behind me.

The red sitting room is filled with four wooden chairs, a low table, and a sideboard holding a few lamps, leaving barely enough room to maneuver between the furniture. The space seems even smaller with Godmother Twelve's imposing figure standing behind a chair. She surveys me with her normal detached expression. Her black dress is immaculate, her black hair in a perfect braided crown around her head.

I grab onto her presence like a lifeline. *Of course! I couldn't tell Godmother Eight about the secret tunnel because she wouldn't listen to me. Godmother Twelve will know what to do. She'll know what it means.* "I'm so glad you're here. I have so much to tell you."

"I've heard. More trips to the market. You and the prince disappearing for hours. I thought you were smarter than that." Her hands tighten on the chair's back.

My relief vanishes. "Y—you told me to keep up

appearances."

"Once again, you completely misunderstand my simple instructions." She gestures to the chair across from her. "Sit."

I perch on the edge of the hard seat. The details of our conversation are hazy, but I thought I was doing what she wanted. I rub my hands together, trying to warm my icy fingertips. "I'm sorry, I thought—I'm sorry."

"Aryanna." Her voice softens and she settles into her chair, leaning over to take my hands. "My child. I'm the one who's sorry. I've been forced to be harsh with you when I don't want to be. I haven't been as affectionate over the years as I should have. I regret that. There's many things I wish I could go back and change, but we're pinning so many hopes on you. It's a great burden." She sighs.

I squeeze her hands. "Forgive me. I know how much you care for me. How hard you've worked all these years. I won't let you down."

"I know you won't. These issues with the Linarians have kept me busy, but I'm doing everything I can to help you behind the scenes. And now that Vivia has recovered, she can guide you. The time to act will soon be upon us, and we're counting on you to fulfill your role."

The words leave me oddly hollow, the expected burst of pride missing. *I'm just tired.*

"Once the royals and everyone with claims to the throne are eliminated, you'll have everything you've ever dreamed of."

My blood freezes. *Eliminated ... as in killed?* They've never said we would kill anyone. I'm not so innocent to assume there won't be casualties, but they always said the royal family would be imprisoned, not executed. Or did they? The Godmothers have always been vague about how the actual takeover will be accomplished. *Was this the plan all along?*

"Now tell me what you've been doing since we last spoke."

My mind is a blank canvas. Images from the past few days briefly color the surface, then drown in a sea of red blood. *I don't want to hurt the king and queen. And Nicolas—she can't kill Nicolas.* "I've been to the marketplace," I offer feebly.

"Yes, yes. I know. You're very fond of leaving the palace. I guess it's to be expected. You've always been driven to distraction, even at the villa."

I twist my hands together in my lap. "There's a lot to see. Everyone and everything in the world passes through Floren."

"I'm sure it feels that way." Her lips press together into thin white lines. "It seems grand and exciting, like the center of the world. But Floren is an illusion. It's too busy admiring itself to care about anything or anyone else. The world would be better off if we burned it to the ground, and the royal family with it."

Her anger throws me off balance, making my temper flare in kind. My instinct is to defend Floren, but I fight to control my emotions. Right now, I need to figure out what's going on.

Why is she so desperate to get control of a kingdom she despises? Shouldn't a good ruler want to protect the kingdom, not destroy it? Nicolas loves Floren more than anything in the world. If he knew about the Godmothers, he would try to find a way to resolve things peacefully, and I know it's not because he's afraid to fight. Look at the tensions with Linaria. The king and queen had every right to be offended when the delegation walked out of the negotiations, but instead of escalating things, they're trying to avoid war at all costs because it would hurt the people and the kingdom. *What does she really want?*

"Godmother Twelve ..." I hesitate, not sure what to say. "You're so respected and admired here. Can't you find a way to make peace between Floren and the Godmothers?"

"Never." Her eyes burn, and her face hardens. She grips the arms of the chair as she leans forward. "They have to pay for their crimes."

Goosebumps break out on my arms in the face of her scorching rage. I tilt away until my back presses against the wood, trying to put distance between us.

In the blink of an eye, she's back in control. "If peace was so easily obtained, don't you think I would have tried? Nay, there can be no peace between us. They've made that clear." She steeples her fingers, tapping them against her chin. "You know they stole the kingdoms from the Godmothers through deceit and murder. When we tried to negotiate a cease fire, they attacked. Since then, they've waged war on us. Sending spies and assassins to hunt us down. It's only because I'm on the Council that I've been able to keep us all safe. The king and queen have fooled everyone. Nobody would believe me if I told them all the horrors we've faced over the years."

That doesn't match the tales they've told me about the king and queen. Something isn't right. "What about the prisoners that disappeared? Who are they?" At her blank look, I add, "The ones you told Godmother Eight about when we were in the carriage."

"Allies of ours. Like your friend." Her eyes narrow.

"Gaia says you've developed feelings for the prince. That you talk about him constantly."

My head snaps back. *Gaia betrayed me?* "I thought you didn't know her."

"She's been part of my network for years."

No—Godmother Twelve didn't know who Gaia was when I mentioned her, I'm sure of it. Was she lying then, or is she lying now?

"Perhaps I made a mistake involving you. Mayhap it's time you return to the villa."

I try to work through the thoughts crowding my mind, each shrieking for attention. *The Godmother is right to be angry if I disobeyed her. But she told me to keep up appearances and continue going on outings with Nicolas. She says I misunderstood, but she didn't explain. She never explains. Now she wants to send me away. I know she's lying about Gaia, but why? What else has she lied about? She says the king and queen have done horrible things, but what if that's a lie too?*

Every conversation with the Godmother leaves me more tangled up than before. False friend or not, Gaia would never treat me this way. She would try to understand what I'm feeling and offer guidance, but ultimately she'd let me decide what I want to do.

There's no compassion or sympathy in the Godmother; she's all sharp edges and haughtiness. *Does she care about me at all? What does she really want from me if I'm so useless?* She ignores me until it's time to berate me. Even when I'm doing what she wants, she tells me I'm wrong. Every interaction is about what she wants from me.

I look at Godmother Twelve with fresh eyes. It's all so clear now. Godmother Twelve doesn't care if I live or die, as long as she gets revenge on Floren and the other provinces. I'm a tool for the Godmothers—and nothing else. Any kindness she's shown me is another part of her lies designed to manipulate me.

My stomach drops to the floor. If the royal family overthrew the Godmothers in her lifetime, how is it possible that nobody knows who she is? If she ruled Floren, then someone, somewhere would identify her. She could never hide in plain sight on the Council.

I'm the biggest fool that's ever walked the land. Everything the Godmothers told me is a lie. The Godmothers don't have a claim on Floren. They're greedy, power-hungry schemers trying to steal something that doesn't belong to them.

I can't let that happen. There must be a way to stop them.

This is bigger than me. Floren must stay safe. I have to protect Nicolas and his parents at all costs. I can't show any weakness in front of the Godmothers. Not now. Not when it could mean the demise of us all.

I square my shoulders and look Godmother Twelve in the eye, fighting to keep the bitterness out of my voice. "I want to stay here. To help you, as you've trained me to do all my life. Tell me what the plan is, so I'll be ready."

"You'll know when the time comes."

"Please." I let some of my eagerness show. "I need to prepare too. Nicol—the prince is very careful. I've seen him fight. If I can take him by surprise, then I have a chance to k— kill him. But if I'm not ready, he may escape. Live to threaten your rule again. He's very popular with the people. They would rally behind him."

"You would kill your prince?"

Those amber eyes staring at me make it hard to think. "To serve the Godmothers, I would do anything. Whatever it takes." I hold my breath.

She studies me, the minutes ticking by. "All in good time. For now, follow Vivia's instructions. We'll be watching you."

The hair on the back of my neck rises. *She knows. That I'm starting to doubt the Godmothers. That I could betray them.*

I don't know where the knowledge comes from, but it rings true. My time is growing short, if it's not already gone. The Godmothers will move quickly, getting rid of me at their first opportunity. I have some protection in my ruse as Princess Aryanna, but it won't last long. All it takes is one accidental fall down the stairs, one wrong turn in the marketplace. I'm sure they'll have alibis in place so my murder can't be traced back to them. Until then, they'll be watching my every move, making sure I don't reveal their plans. Nicolas and his parents are in even greater danger.

Godmother Twelve reaches out and cups my cold cheek with her hand. "So many years you've been in our care. So much time and effort to bring you here." She stands. "I'll call on you when I need you."

When she needs to put an end to me. I shove the worry aside. Nicolas and his family are the ones who need protection. I can take care of myself, disappear if I need to. But I have to make sure they're safe first.

She pauses at the door. "Keep sharp. There are secrets all over this palace. You never know what's hiding behind a door."

The breath leaves my lungs. *Does she know about the secret tunnel? Was that a warning she knows what Nicolas and Lia are doing?*

Godmother Eight reappears, grabbing my arm and propelling me down the hallway. I stumble on the carpet and stairs as my mind frantically tries to decode Godmother Twelve's parting words.

If she's aware of the tunnels, nobody is safe. They could walk into a trap at any moment. Are they going to use the tunnel tonight? I have to warn them.

As we reach my rooms, one of the queen's ladies calls out to Godmother Eight. "Lady Vivia, a moment if you please. There's an issue with tomorrow's schedule."

Godmother Eight gives her a radiant smile. "Let me see to my mistress, and then I'll be right there."

Her grip tightens as she drags me through the doorway and pushes me toward the couch. "Stay here."

I keep my face blank as she storms out. The click of the lock echoes throughout the room.

This is my chance. I can warn them about the Godmothers and get back before she knows I was gone.

I spare a moment to look longingly at my bed, then head to the closet to dig out my trousers and tunic.

28

Thank the heavens, the suite below mine has a nice, wide balcony. I release the dangling bedsheet and drop lightly into a crouch. A glance inside confirms the room is vacant; a bent pin takes care of the locked door. I slip through the room and into the hallway, making a note of the location for my return trip. No doubt Godmother Eight stationed someone to watch my door while she's attending to other matters.

Finding Gaia would be my first choice, but she's disappeared since Godmother Eight returned. Where would Nicolas be at this hour? Not in bed—or if he is, then my excursion will be for naught, since I'm sure the Godmothers have spies watching his chambers. No, I better hope he's as restless as I am. The likely possibilities are the secret passage, strategizing with Captain Rossi, or with his parents. I'll check the passage first as my best chance to catch him or Lia alone.

If he told Lia about our kiss, I'm definitely getting stabbed. I hope I can fight her off long enough to warn her about the Godmothers.

I keep the hood of my cloak on as I hurry through the palace to the secret room. After a few moments fumbling in the dark, I locate the trigger stone, stepping inside as soon as the doorway swings open.

And come face-to-face with Lia.

She snarls, "You!" A knife flies into her hand.

Burn it. I hold my dagger in a defensive stance, trying not to appear threatening, but ready to defend myself if needed. "Wait! I already know about the tunnel and the supplies."

Lia's knife lowers a hairsbreadth. "How'd you find out?"

I need her to trust me if she's going to believe me about the Godmothers. "By accident. Nicolas didn't say anything. He doesn't know I know. I haven't told anyone else." It might be a mistake telling her that, but one of us has to make a leap of faith first, and Lia isn't capable of it.

She glares—a marked improvement. Usually she looks like she wants to kill me. *I think she's warming up to me.*

I press my advantage. "What's going on, Lia? It must be dangerous with all the secrecy. Are you planning an attack?"

"You're even more clay-brained than I thought." She flicks her red braid over her shoulder. "Go back to your rooms, and forget you ever found this place." The knife disappears into her jacket.

She definitely likes me. "Please, I have to find Nicolas. He's in danger."

She snorts. "And *you're* going to protect him? Go to bed, Princess."

I eye her, trying to decide if she'll listen to me or dismiss the threat. *I have to try.* "You need to warn Nicolas. There's a group called the Godmothers that—"

The secret door slides open. Lia mutters an oath, shoving me behind her as a woman limps inside.

Gaia does a double take. "Aryanna! What are you doing here?" Her spotless blush-pink dress is a stark contrast to Lia's tattered clothing.

Lia says, "Never you mind. Where is he?"

I grab her shoulder. "Lia, Gaia. Listen to me. The Godmothers are trying to overthrow the kingdom. They're going to kill the royal family and anyone with a claim to the throne."

Gaia sucks in a breath.

The redhead shoves me away. "Are you trying to wake up the whole palace? Tell me later. We have a more urgent matter right now."

A cloaked figure stumbles into the small space. The hood falls back to reveal a young man made old by hardships. His dirty, pinched face is creased with deep lines. Every movement is painful, judging by the winces and slow, careful movements.

Lia utters another oath and moves forward to support him. "Hurry up and get down there."

For a second, I think she's speaking to me, but it's Gaia who opens the trapdoor and climbs down. Lia waits until we hear her splash down at the bottom, then helps the man onto the ladder.

Just as she closes the trapdoor, a woman's angry voice echoes down the passageway.

We freeze, staring at each other.

The door is open. They'll find the secret room when they turn the corner. I have to stop them. I draw my dagger and dash toward the entrance.

Lia springs forward, smashing the hilt of her knife on

my head. Lights explode in my vision, and I sink to the ground with a groan.

"Shut up," she hisses. "Stay out of the way."

There's a loud scraping noise. I hold my head, every heartbeat a pounding drum inside my skull. A thought struggles to find its way to the surface. *Danger. Woman. Discovery.* I roll to my hands and knees, swallowing down the bile burning my throat. Everything is a blur. I blink, trying to clear my vision. Slowly, slowly, the wall swims into focus.

I don't know how long it takes to crawl across the room. Finally, my fingers find the right stone and press it. I fall through the opening as the wall slides open, scraping my palms on the floor.

The hallway is empty.

My strength gives out, and I collapse again, rolling onto my back. Time passes in a haze. I shiver uncontrollably for what feels like hours, then slowly the chills leave me, and I drift into blessed numbness. Footsteps echo down the passage.

Nicolas's face comes into view above me, appearing a bit smudged around the edges. "Aryanna? What are you doing here? What happened? You're freezing."

He scoops me up, wrapping the edges of my cloak around me.

I try to say something, but the movement brings my nausea rushing back. I press my lips together and breathe through my nose, crushing myself against his chest to soak in his heat. My thoughts fade in and out as he carries me through the palace.

Nicolas fumbles with a door, then kicks it closed behind him. He carries me across the room to a roaring fire and gently rubs my hands between his. Pain lances through my body as it slowly warms.

"Aryanna? Where are you hurt?"

"Hmm?" I try to focus on him, but his face keeps sliding away.

Nicolas. I need to tell him something. The words flutter through my mind, then disappear into the darkness. *What happened?* "Lia. Godmothers." *What was I saying?* "Where's Lia? She ran after …"

He grips my shoulders tightly, his face inches from mine. "Aryanna, please. Tell me what happened. Where's Lia?"

The pressure clears my head for a moment. "A woman was coming. Lia hit me and ran out." I weakly push him toward the door. "Go. Help her. She's in danger."

Nicolas curses under his breath as he looks between me and the door. "Lia won't trust anybody else. And they won't know where to look." He brushes his fingers down my cheek and wraps a blanket around me. "Stay here, you'll be safe. I'll send Gaia and one of the doctors to help you until I can get back."

His footsteps run across the carpet to the door. Silence.

I close my eyes as everything goes blurry, my head rolling to the side. I slump down.

As my muscles thaw, the pounding in my head increases to fill my entire existence. Waves of pain with no end in sight. The surges gradually recede until I'm left with a dull ache. I sit up carefully, testing every inch, lest I slip back into darkness.

This can only be Nicolas's room. While the rest of the palace is gilded with decorations on every surface, the walls in here are a light-green color, similar to my suite, broken up

with an occasional tapestry depicting forests or scenes from
Floren. A wide table to the side is covered with bits of
machinery in various states of assembly, tools scattered
among the pieces. The furniture is heavy and comfortable
looking, not meant to impress. The fireplace is large enough
to roast an ox. A collection of ancient weapons covers the
longest wall.

My muddled thoughts trip over each other as I try to
focus. The Godmothers have surely noted my absence by
now. If they catch me, I'm dead.

I should leave.

The thought hits me like a thunderbolt. Not only his
room, but the palace. Panic shoves everything away except
the urgent demand to be gone from here. My muscles scream
with the need to move. To flee. Terror pushes me to my feet,
and I stagger to the door.

I slip out of the room and make my way toward the
servants' staircase at the end of the hall. After a few steps,
it's clear I'm in no shape to get to the tunnel unnoticed.
Leaning against the walls is the only way I can stay upright.
Every few feet, dizziness sets in, and I nearly pass out. It's
slow going down the narrow stairway.

After two floors, I know I can't go much further, the
bruises on my arms and legs already aching from my
frequent falls. Soon I'll do the Godmothers' work for them
and break my neck. I crawl into a hallway and manage to
push open the nearest door, finding a small bedroom.

I curl up in the bottom of the dusty armoire and close the
door, promising myself I'll only rest for a few minutes.

My eyes slide closed, and I tumble into oblivion.

29

I bolt upright, then groan and put a hand to my head. A large knot on the side of my skull throbs in time with my pulse. The previous evening's events dribble back to me in broken fragments: the secret room, the unseen woman, Lia's attack.

I tug the cloak tighter around me, remembering the way Nicolas ran off. *What did I say to him?* It's all so hazy. My throbbing head won't let me put together the events.

Gaia was with Lia last night. She's caught up in whatever dangerous game Nicolas and Lia are playing, and now I am too. I ignore the heaviness in my stomach that they've all been working together and purposefully kept me out of their confidence.

Everyone is not what they seem, including me. To think I was willing to throw everything away for them. I shake my head, immediately regretting the jarring movement.

I could tell Godmother Twelve what I know and show her I'm loyal. Get back into her trust. Pay back the Florens for all the anger and hurt at being left out, being lied to. My injured pride screams for vengeance. But I can't. Even knowing they're up to something, I still can't bring myself to betray them.

The siren call of freedom is strong, but I need to make sure Lia is safe and that they're properly warned about the Godmothers. Then I'll slip away with a clear conscience.

Gaia is still my first choice to seek out, but I don't know where she'll be. I have no idea where Lia is, and I doubt she'd take me seriously anyway. That leaves Nicolas or his parents. Too risky, I'd definitely be spotted by the Godmothers' network of spies before I can flee.

A letter. I'll write a letter to Gaia explaining everything. She can pass on my warning after I'm gone.

My mood lightens at having a plan. I make my way through the palace, keeping to the shadows and unused areas. My tunic and trousers will draw too much attention, and right now I need to remain unnoticed as long as I can. From the maps I've memorized, I navigate to a small library, complete with a writing desk in the corner. I quickly scribble out as much as I know about the Godmothers' plans, splattering ink across the page in my haste. *Now to deliver it.* One of the servants must know where Gaia's room is. I'll have to hide it there myself; the information is too important to trust to a stranger.

It's frustratingly difficult to find a servant to ask; they've all disappeared. Nobles crowd the hallways. Godmother Twelve and Lord Franco come around a corner, and I duck behind a staircase before they can spot me. She seems to be in a good mood, her tight smile broader, her gestures a bit looser.

It's a sign. Every moment I'm in the palace increases my chances of the Godmothers finding me. It's time to throw caution to the wind. If I work quickly enough and luck is on my side, I can confirm Lia and Nicolas are safe, then leave before I'm caught.

I force myself to count to one hundred after Godmother Twelve is out of sight, then make my way to the kitchens. The room is blissfully hot from the three giant wall ovens bellowing heat. Every surface is covered with piles of vegetables and shining platters stacked with dishes. There's hardly room to spit, but somehow the staff moves around each other without causing a disaster. I scan the faces, looking for someone familiar.

A young maid spots me as and rushes over. "My lady, you shouldn't be in here."

"I'm trying to find Gaia's rooms. Do you know where they are?"

A hush falls over the kitchen.

The maid's face goes pale. "Please. Go." She ushers me toward the door.

I plant my feet. "I'm not leaving until I find her."

A footman takes my arm. "We can't help you." His eyes bore into mine, and he subtly inclines his head in a silent message.

I let him lead me out of the kitchen as the other servants watch.

He gestures toward one passageway and mouths, "Go to the end."

I nod my thanks, then go the way he indicated. The few open doors reveal a series of storerooms, then plain bedrooms. The way narrows until my fingertips brush the walls on each side as I walk. A myriad of twists and turns ends in front of a thick wooden door. I pull it open to find Gaia, Nicolas, and two women I don't recognize huddled over a shape in a corner.

I catch of glimpse of Lia's face among the blankets, drained and pinched in pain. She moans as one woman presses on her side.

"Is she all right?" *Foolish question, of course she's not.* "What happened? Did that woman do this to her? Who was it?"

"Aryanna." Nicolas looks stunned, then his face turns stony. He strides over and stops in front of me, crossing his arms. "Why did you leave my room? I told you to wait there."

"I—I was worried they'd find me. I was trying to get somewhere safe."

"We wasted time looking for you."

I wrap my arms around my middle. "I'm sorry."

"You were followed to the tunnels. That's why Lia got hurt. She was protecting you by leading them away."

My head shoots up. "Impossible." *Or is it? Did someone follow me?* I wasn't paying attention when I went to the passage, I was too intent on warning them about the Godmothers. Which was the perfect opportunity to lead the Godmothers right to them. The truth hits me like a punch to guts. *The Godmothers must have known I would warn them and followed me. It is my fault.*

Nicolas says, "If you hadn't gone to the tunnel last night, none of this would have happened."

Lia's weak voice still manages to sound hard enough to break rocks. "You idiot. She didn't do anything."

Nicolas hurries over and kneels next to his friend. "You're awake."

"Hard to stay asleep when you're yelling loud enough to wake the dead."

Watching the affection between them breaks my heart.

Not because I'm jealous of their love for each other, but seeing it reminds me how alone I really am. When I leave the palace, I leave my entire world behind. The Godmothers may be villains, but they're the only family I've ever known. Now I'm their sworn enemy, and they'll stop at nothing to get their revenge. When the people at the palace learn the whole truth about me, I'll be nothing more than a traitorous spy who failed at her mission. Even the individuals who may look past my lies like Gaia will be lost to me, since I can't risk my safety or theirs to see them again.

And Nicolas … *No, I can't bear to think about him.*

I run out of the room and lean against the wall, burying my face in my hands.

Gaia follows me. She puts an arm around my shoulder. "He doesn't mean it. He's lashing out because he's scared. Two of the people he loves most in the world were hurt and in danger, and there was nothing he could do. Lia was in bad shape when he found her. Then, when you weren't in his room, he went into a frenzy. I've never seen him so frightened."

I accept her explanation with dull resignation. It's probably true, but it won't matter when he finds who I really am. "I can help Lia. I have medicines, and I know how to treat wounds." One last good deed before I vanish.

"The doctors have already seen her, and they're confident she'll recover." She turns me toward the kitchens. "Go. Wait for me in your bedroom. Vivia will be looking for you, and she can't find you here."

She's right. The Godmothers won't stop searching the palace unless they know I'm gone. They might stumble on to Lia in their hunt. I'll have to make it obvious I've left.

I blink the tears away as I silently say goodbye to my

friend, then press the letter into Gaia's hand. "When you tell him about the Godmothers, don't say it came from me. I don't know what they're planning, but it'll be soon. You have to save them."

Before she can respond, I run, not looking back. I don't stop until I've reached my bedroom. In a flurry, I throw clothing and jewels into a small bag, then pull on a simple gray dress and cloak to cover my trousers and tunic until I'm safely out of the city. Sadly, my treasured medicine chest is too large to carry. I settle for wrapping my favorite vials and jars in a nightshift, then tucking them down in the clothing. I toss more clothes out of the closet and open drawers to make it clear someone came through here in a hurry. Combined with the missing items, the Godmothers will know I've fled and look for me outside the palace. Once I'm on the road, I'll have to hide my trail well to avoid capture.

The tunnel is compromised. I'll drop the bag out the window to the bushes below and pick it up on my way out the gates. Stealing a horse from the stables will be simple enough. Once I'm outside the walls, I'll disappear.

There's a hollow feeling in my chest as I glance around the room, searching for anything I've missed.

One last thing. I place the sapphire dagger Nicolas gave me on the bed. It's a beautiful weapon, and it hurts to leave it behind, but I can't take it. I don't deserve it. I hope he recognizes it for the apology I mean it to be.

If only Lia hadn't knocked me on the head last night, I could have helped her. Then she wouldn't have gotten hurt, and I could have left the palace without this weight on my heart. But yesterday is done. All I can do is my best for today, and plan for tomorrow. At least Nicolas and his parents are safe now; Gaia will see to that.

Swiping my sleeve across my eyes, I pull my shoulders back and head to the window.

The door bangs open.

Godmother Twelve sweeps in, followed by ten guards. More crowd the hallway behind them. They lower swords and crossbows in my direction. I drop the bag and throw my hands in front of me as I back away, ice running through my veins.

The Godmother points at me. "Arrest her."

30

The guards push me into the cell without ceremony. My tired feet stumble over each other, and I tumble to the stone floor, reigniting the pain from my earlier bruises. The door slams closed. I curl up in the corner, putting my chin on my knees and wrapping my arms around my legs.

I always thought a dungeon would be a damp, dank place smelling of rot and echoing with the moans of people being tortured. But Floren's dungeons are prime accommodations by those standards. Aside from the stale smell, lack of windows, and the locked door, there's not much to complain about. Fresh straw and rushes strewn on the ground. A long slab bolted to the wall works for a chair or bed, a folded blanket and a small pillow set on its surface. A chamber pot is discreetly tucked under the bench. Thin slits above the door let in light. Plenty of room to stand and move around. A well-appointed cell as far as dungeons go.

I just wish I knew why I was in here.

My pleas to the guards fell on deaf ears. I was quite the spectacle as they marched me through the palace, but none of the witnesses called out or provided any clues as to why I was arrested. It's maddening not knowing.

Godmother Twelve is very clever. She planted me in the kingdom to pose as the Cabriaren princess without Cabriare knowing or Floren suspecting anything. That was a monumental feat in itself. Now she's turned Floren against me when they were thoroughly convinced of my role.

She's taken another approach to getting rid of me. Did she tell everyone I'm an imposter? Accuse me of conspiring with Floren's enemies? Convince them that Cabriare has turned against them? It couldn't be a small crime. Floren would never risk a war with Cabriare without solid evidence of serious misconduct.

Not that it matters; I'm doomed no matter what. My warnings will go unheeded now that everyone knows I'm a traitor. Gaia and Lia won't warn Nicolas, or he'll dismiss the threat as more lies, and soon it'll be too late. Yes, Godmother Twelve is very, very clever.

I touch the few pins still jammed haphazardly into my hair. They can be used to pick the lock, but there were at least four guards stationed in the hallway and another three sitting in the small room at the entrance to the dungeon. I'm good at taking on multiple attackers, but not that good. Nonetheless, I pull them out and straighten them, hiding some in my clothing and keeping a few at hand.

After some hours pass, the door opens, and a guard sets a tray of food on the floor. I settle on the wooden bench and survey my options. Slices of thick brown bread full of nuts and dried fruit, chunks of baked pumpkin, a handful of figs, and a large mug of water. After testing for poisons and other drugs, I force myself to eat the items one by one to keep up my strength. The food is well prepared, but each bite turns to dust in my mouth. It's hard to swallow around the lump in my throat.

Another guard comes for the tray after I've finished. He ignores my questions, leaving a pitcher of water and the mug behind.

The hours melt into each other. At regular intervals during the rest of the evening and into the next morning, the guards bring more food or replace the water. I pace around my cell, kicking the rushes to work out my anger. I try going through my training poses to settle my mind, but it keeps chasing after what-nows and what-ifs. Finally, I give up and lie on the bench, staring at the ceiling as my thoughts whirl in a maelstrom of worries.

Gaia slips into the room. "Oh, Aryanna, I'm so sorry. I never thought it would come to this."

I run over and embrace her. "Thank the heavens you're here. Do you know why I was arrested?"

"Serafina outed you as an imposter. She had evidence you aren't the real Cabriare princess."

The way she said it—I look at her sharply. "You knew?"

Gaia pushes up her sleeve. High on her arm is a small tattoo of a rose surrounded by a crown of thorns.

The Godmothers' symbol.

I shoot away, pressing my back against the cold stone wall. "Who are you?"

A wistful smile crosses her face as she settles on the bench. "It's too much to hope you remember me; you were only a toddler. You were the sweetest girl. Always smiling and laughing. Carrying that little wooden doll with you everywhere. It broke my heart to leave you behind, but I barely survived escaping myself." She rubs her injured leg absentmindedly.

"You're a Godmother." My stomach twists. *The Thirteenth Godmother. This whole time, she knew who I was.* "You're working with them! You put me in here."

"No, sweetling! I would never." She makes a motion toward me, dropping her hands when I cringe back. "I was part of the Godmothers, it's true. But when we took you, I realized how cruel we were. That we were the ones who needed to be stopped."

I wrap my arms around my middle. "Took me?"

"Your parents, they're not who you think. You are the niece of the Queen of Cabriare. Your mother was her twin sister. Your father was a Patrizio. The Godmothers killed your parents and kidnapped you, and I was too late to stop them. Everyone in Cabriare believes you're dead. I couldn't stay after that."

My mouth falls open, and I drop next to her on the bench. *This sounds like some ridiculous folk tale, but Gaia is serious.*

"We called ourselves the Godmothers because we saw ourselves as mothers over all the people. Really, we were arrogant, infantile women who thought we could help the world by controlling it. And Serafina fooled us, just like she fooled you. Although I imagine the other Godmothers know or suspect the real purpose of the organization by now." She grimaces. "You've heard of the Ghibellines?"

The Council meeting flashes through my mind. "Once. There was a war between them and Floren?"

"Not just Floren. The Ghibellines attacked Aemilia, Cabriare, Ranuvia, Flaminia, even Linaria, leaving devastation everywhere they went. Floren is where they were finally stopped and defeated once and for all. Serafina's family occupied a small estate on Floren's border. The

206

Ghibellines razed it in one of their raids, killing everyone. Serafina and her little sister only survived because they were in the forest with their nanny when the attack happened. The nanny abandoned them and fled. The two girls hid in the woods for weeks. They thought the king would save them. Tragically, a pack of wild dogs attacked her sister, and she died in Serafina's arms. After, Serafina walked to the neighboring town four days away. Nobody there even knew the estate had been attacked."

How horrible to lose everything and not be able to do anything about it. She must have felt so helpless.

"Serafina blamed Floren. By leaving protection to the villages, the border was vulnerable, especially to a force like the Ghibellines. The king was too slow in sending troops to reinforce the locals. She vowed to make the kingdom a safer place so nobody's family would suffer the same fate. At least, that's what she claims the Godmothers are for. All she really cares about is getting revenge on the royals."

"But surely the king and queen are too young to have been involved in what happened."

"It matters not. Serafina is cruel. Cold. She's waited decades for revenge. If she can't get her justice on the original perpetrators, their successors will do. She won't stop with Floren. Over the years, her lust for vengeance has grown to include all the kingdoms that failed to stop the Ghibellines. I don't tell you this to excuse her behavior, but because I don't want you to go down the same twisted path. There are hurts in life we must learn to let go lest they ruin us."

Before I knew Nicolas, I'm not sure I could have understood how the pain of losing someone could drive you to such a dark place. But now I can glimpse a little of what drives Godmother Twelve. *If Nicolas were killed … I shudder.*

"After I left the Godmothers, I knew I had to do something to stop Serafina. She's too well shielded to confront directly. I came here to protect the royal family without alerting her to my presence. It took many years, but eventually I built up a network of my own. We smuggle out the prisoners the Godmothers have falsely imprisoned and provide refugees from other kingdoms with provisions to find safety and make a new life."

That's why they have the supplies in the tunnel. Not for an army, but for victims. A sense of lightness fills me, while my heart is heavy for doubting their motives. *Nicolas is right to reject me; he deserves better.*

"Eventually, I recruited Lia to my cause. And she brought Nicolas."

I try to absorb everything, each revelation bigger than the next. *Gaia is the Thirteenth Godmother. Nicolas will believe her; he'll be safe. She knew I was an imposter the whole time. She knew about my real parents. Why didn't she tell me earlier?*

"Why are you telling me all this? Why are you here?"

"I'm going to help you escape."

At first I think I misheard her. "You're going to get me out of the dungeon?" *But she knows I'm really an imposter, that I was going to help the Godmothers overthrow the royal family.*

"Of course, sweetling. It's not your fault you were put into this situation, and you would never harm the king or queen. Weren't you trying to leave the palace when you were caught?"

Yes, I was running away again. Just like after I kissed Nicolas. I never thought myself weak, but I've proven I'm a coward at my core.

Tears well up. "Will you tell Nicolas goodbye for me? And how sorry I am?"

"I will. But one day you'll see him again. Promise me you'll tell him you love him."

"No—no. I don't. I was playing my part. It meant nothing."

This time I don't resist when Gaia takes my hands in hers.

"Everyone can see it when you and Nicolas are together. You love him."

My resistance collapses at her kindness and my shoulders droop. "It doesn't matter, he hates me. You heard what he said."

"He loves you. He was just scared and lashed out. I'm sure he already regrets his harsh words. He didn't mean it."

He did. She doesn't know I deserved everything he said and more.

"I have to leave." Gaia looks at the door. "In fifteen minutes or so, a guard will come and open the door, then walk away. The dungeon will be clear. Take a uniform and any supplies you need from the tunnel, then leave the city and head north. I'll meet you at the first farmhouse at dawn." She squeezes my hands. "There's so much more I need to tell you, but we don't have time. Be safe, sweetling."

"Wait!" I clutch her hand. "What's my name? My *real* name?" The longing is thick in my voice. My heart leaps into my throat, needing her to answer.

Her eyes go sad. "It's Aurelia Rosa." She kisses me on the cheek, then disappears through the door, shutting it softly behind her.

Aurelia Rosa! Golden Rose. My hand flies to my mouth as happiness floods me. *I have a name. My own name, not hers. And parents. There are people out there who can tell me about them. I can figure out who I was. Who I am.*

Gaia is Godmother Thirteen. I wish I could remember her. A few shadows flicker in my memory, but it's hard to tell if they're real or wishful thinking. Her network must be powerful to help prisoners escape on a regular basis. But powerful enough to overcome the other Godmothers? That I doubt. Godmother Twelve has spun a vast network over the years; it seems inconceivable that she can be defeated.

I can't keep still, knowing my freedom is close at hand. I pace the room, testing the door every few minutes.

On my next pass, I stumble when the door opens at my touch. I rush out, but there's nobody in sight. The guard's room at the end of the dungeon is vacant.

The hallways are eerily empty as I make my way to the passage with the tunnel. *How did she manage that?* I navigate the tunnel by touch, breathing a sigh of relief at the small glowing light coming from the storage area. Someone left a small lamp burning next to a satchel sitting on a crate.

I tear into the bag. Food, smallclothes, some knives. My hand freezes when I come across the beautiful dagger Nicolas gave to me a lifetime ago. I run my finger across the sapphire, remembering how his eyes lit up when I opened the box.

Everything changed when I met him, even though I didn't know it at the time. The prince had every right to snub me when I first arrived, but instead he welcomed me. Teased me. Became my friend despite my best efforts to push him away. He opened my eyes to the world and helped me discover the truth about the Godmothers and myself. I fell in love with his kindness and humor and curiosity.

I grip the hilt and set my jaw. *I have to save him.*

There's only one way to truly protect Nicolas: I have to stop Godmother Twelve. Now.

While Godmother Twelve is here, the royal family is in danger. Gaia can't know all the preparations they've made in the years she's been gone. Godmother Twelve makes plans within plans and keeps those secrets close. She's the heart of the conspiracy against Floren. Without her, they'll fail. Then Gaia can dismantle the organization.

If I stay, I'll get caught. It's inevitable. There's too many people at the palace to avoid being recognized, and with my public arrest, they'll know I've escaped. Everyone is a potential spy for the Godmothers. They may not bother with taking me alive this time. Nobody will question a traitor who's killed trying to escape.

This is my only chance to leave. Gaia won't be able to get me out again.

It doesn't matter what happens to me as long as they're safe.

Locating and stopping Godmother Twelve will take time. A guard outfit will make it easier to avoid notice when I'm moving around the palace. Most people will only see the uniform and not the face attached to it. I quickly change, cutting a hole in the pocket for access to the sapphire dagger, which I strap to my thigh. A strip from my discarded clothing serves as a wrap around my waist, holding the other knives out of sight under the jacket.

My boots are passable, but my hair isn't. The uniform doesn't have a hat, and most guards wear their hair in a small club. My hair is too long, it'll attract attention. I wince, then pull my braid straight out and saw at the base of it, biting my lips as the blade slices through the strands. My head is oddly light and off-balance, my neck springy. I tie what remains of my ebony waves back with another scrap of fabric. Not ideal, but it should help me hide my identity long enough to accomplish my task.

One deep breath, then I climb the stairs.

Let the hunt begin.

32

Disused hallways and empty rooms provide cover as I dart through the palace. My chest is tight, the blood pounding through my veins. It's like right before a fight multiplied by a hundred. A thousand. There is no tomorrow for me. Knowing this is my last chance to save Nicolas and his parents makes every decision critical. I can't afford any mistakes.

There's a sleeping draught in my medicine chest. If I can slip it into Godmother Twelve's evening tea, we can smuggle her through the secret tunnel and out of the palace without raising an alarm. Gaia and Nicolas can spread rumors about "Lady Serafina" being called away on urgent business.

Ugh, that's a terrible plan. There's no way I can make it to my rooms and out again without being caught, even if I climb around the outside walls, and I'd likely break my neck trying. But I should tell Gaia about the sleeping draught anyway. She can figure out a way to retrieve it and put it to good use.

If only I could tell Nicolas everything, convince him of the danger. He would make sure his parents are protected. The more people who know, the better. But he's so angry. He won't listen to me. Even if he did, he'd never believe me. But he trusts Gaia. Nicolas will believe her, and he can sway his parents.

I shouldn't have wasted all that time in the dungeon. We could be working together right now. But I'll find her. We'll stop the Godmothers and make sure this never happens again.

First thing is to alert Gaia that I'm staying, and we need to act now. I'll start by watching Godmother Twelve from the shadows. Figure out how they're planning to attack and ways to prevent it. Look for opportunities to capture her. Track who she's talking to and ensure she doesn't harm the royal family. Find out who her allies are—until I get caught. Knowing the Godmother's contacts will be useful. Gaia can track the spies to more spies and rid Floren of its pests.

If I can catch Godmother Twelve alone, there are a few techniques Seven taught me that I can use to physically overpower her without hurting her. Unlikely, but worth trying. I won't be able to move her far by myself, so I'll have to have a hiding spot nearby where I can hold her until Gaia's network takes over.

Better, but still not a good plan.

Too bad, it's all I've got.

No matter what happens to me tonight, the Godmothers will threaten Floren no more.

Where would Gaia be? The room where Lia was being treated seems like the most likely place to start. And if Gaia's not there, Lia might be. I grimace at the thought of relying on the redhead to help me, but sometimes you can't

pick your allies. It's important to get the message to Gaia—
even if it means dealing with that stubborn baitfish.

When I reach the kitchen hallway, I utter a curse under
my breath. It's busier than I've ever seen it. Maids bustle in
and out with trays, footmen carry dishes and baskets, and
other servers are laden with bowls of fruit and bottles of
wine. The imposing housekeeper presides over the chaos,
barking orders to ensure everything runs smoothly. It'll be
hours before the hallway quiets down, and I don't have
hours.

I can't wait. I have to risk it.

Pretending to scratch my ear so my arm hides my face, I
walk purposefully down the hall. A few people glance my
way, but nobody seems to pay me any mind in my guard
uniform. I'm barely past the kitchen door when a bump
sends me stumbling forward. Hands grab me from behind,
steadying me.

A woman says, "My apologies! Are you all right?"

Nononononononono.

"I'm fine." I hurry forward, turning my head to the side.

"Here, let—" She claps a hand over her mouth when she
catches sight of my face.

*The freckled maid from my room. The one Vivia
terrorized.*

We lock eyes. Mine pleading, hers shocked. A thousand
emotions flicker over her face, too fast for me to capture,
until it settles into understanding.

"Of course." Her eyes dart behind me, then back. "I'm
needed in the ballroom. The king and queen are there. And
the prince."

I mouth, "Thank you."

She nods, then dashes away.

I walk as quickly as I dare until I reach a corner, then sprint to the small room. A peek inside confirms only Lia and the younger woman from last night are inside.

The redhead pins her eyes on me and snorts. "I should've known you couldn't follow simple directions." Lia looks at her companion. "It's just the mock princess, Margherita. She's harmless."

For the first time in a long while, I feel like smiling. "I see those punctures didn't damage your cheery personality."

She snorts, then clutches her side. "Ow. Shut the door already. Are you trying to get us caught again?"

"You need to get a message to Gaia. I'm staying to help to stop Godmo—Lady Serafina. She's going to kill the royal family. I don't know how, but it'll be soon."

Lia crosses her arms and leans back against the wall. "How do you know?"

She'll never believe my wild tale. It'll only make her distrust me more. "I don't have time to explain, but she's been plotting against Floren for years." I quickly outline my plan. "We need to stop Serafina before it's too late. Please, tell Gaia. She knows the people behind it."

She's unimpressed by my pleas. "What exactly am I supposed to do? Nobody is coming back here tonight. Gaia's in the ballroom with the rest of the staff. Do you expect me to borrow one of your ridiculous dresses and waltz in there? I can't move more than five steps without bleeding to death, not to mention there's probably orders to arrest me on sight."

I turn to her caretaker. "You can go."

"Margherita isn't supposed to be in the palace. Are you going to make her go into the ballroom with all those nobles and guards around? Think that will turn out well?"

Margherita whimpers, cowering against the wall. Her

face goes pale, and a sheen of sweat breaks out across her forehead.

Burn it, she'd faint before she made it through the doorway.

Lia wiggles down, wincing. "If it's that urgent, hide somewhere and seek Gaia out when the ball is over."

"Fine," I snap. "But make sure you tell Gaia and Nicolas when you see them, because I'm going to be dragged back to the dungeon as soon as I leave this room."

"Great, I'll say hi when they throw me in the room next to yours. Until then, I need sleep." She pulls a blanket up to her chin and closes her eyes.

Gah! For a moment, I consider adding to her knife wounds. It would serve her right, the arrogant, annoying, ratsbane! *ARRRGHHHHH!*

I give Margherita a curt nod and slip out of the room before the temptation to strangle Lia becomes irresistible. *Where can I hide until Gaia finishes with the ball? At least I'm spared that torture. Poor Nicolas, he'll have to suffer through making small talk with all those boring people. He'll hate—* I stumble to a stop, my lungs freezing.

Everyone. Together. The ball would be the perfect opportunity to strike. Not just at the royal family, but at all the nobility of Floren. A crippling blow to the rulers that will allow the Godmothers to move in and take over before anyone knew what happened.

The attack. It's tonight. And nobody knows it's coming.

33

After shouting a warning to Lia, I sprint down the hallway, skidding around corners, my mind racing. The guard outfit will get me into the ballroom. The crowd will provide more opportunities to blend in but also to be spotted. I need to find Gaia and figure out the Godmothers' plan fast or we're all doomed.

Every second I'm in the ballroom will work against me. If I'm caught, I'll scream out a warning they're about to be attacked. It'll put everyone on alert, even if they don't believe me. It's not the best solution, but tonight is all about poor planning and desperation.

My heart pounds harder with every step. As I pass the kitchen, I yank a tray filled with plates out of a server's hands, ignoring her curse. Keeping the tray high and my head low, I continue my mad dash through the palace.

The farther I travel, the more people materialize in the hallways. Servants hurry back and forth between the ballroom and the kitchen, laden with trays, dishes, and other odds and ends. They seem to be in a good mood, despite the extra workload. Scattered clusters of nobles dressed in fine silks and flashing jewels stand chatting and drinking from delicate flutes. Guards are stationed throughout the halls. Holding the heavy tray keeps my hands from shaking as I pass them, and I make sure to keep my eyes averted. The noise from the ball reaches me before I round the corner and the open doors come into sight.

The ballroom is transformed from the day Nicolas and I spent here. Chandeliers glimmer with candlelight overhead, sparkling off the gilding on the walls and ceiling. The blue plaster makes the walls disappear into the background, while the gold embellishments shine like stars. Lamps in niches along the wall cast a warm glow. Strains of music float up from the side of the room, the musicians powering to overcome the deafening chatter from the crowd. People fill the space, barely leaving enough room for the dancers swirling in the middle of the room and the buffet tables lining the walls.

My stomach drops. I'll never find Gaia in this. *But I have to try.*

I edge around the room, scanning the crowd for Gaia's short figure and white hair. It's slow going. The crowd seems determined to move against me, making me work for every inch of progress. People knock into me on all sides, threatening to tip the heavy tray. The air is a suffocating mix of perfume and food. My stomach churns, and I concentrate on breathing through my mouth. Colors blur together as nobility and servers blend in a swirling kaleidoscope. Using my elbows and hips, I push through the crowd. *Gaia is here somewhere.* It feels like more people appear in the ballroom every second.

The musicians finish the song with a flourish. On the

dais across the room, the king and queen move to the front of the platform. Tonight, they're every inch the rulers of Floren. King Luka's deep-scarlet robe is trimmed with gold embroidery, while Queen Renata's sweeping gold gown is the perfect complement. It's hard to recognize them as the same people who sat on the carpet and played tiles a lifetime ago.

The majordomo's deep baritone carries across the hushed crowd. "It's time for a toast."

Servers bustle through the room with trays of delicate flutes filled with a light-pink drink. I take advantage of the calm to creep back against the wall and search the servers for Gaia. The nobles pluck the glasses from the passing trays as the king steps forward.

He spreads his arms. "My fellow citizens, we're here to celebrate Floren. Tonight is about remembering who we are. How, by coming together, we defended our kingdom against the Ghibellines. How we …"

His words fade into the background as I concentrate on locating Gaia. There are a few familiar faces in the group, but most people have their backs to me, intent on the king's speech. The crowd shifts forward to reveal a glimpse of Godmother Twelve on the edge of the room. She's changed into an elaborate bright-red dress, her hair pulled into a tight bun instead of its custom braid, her face a portrait of polite interest.

My muscles lock into place, and all I can do is stare. My heart gallops, and my legs shake. I've been so busy planning how to stop her, I didn't consider how it would feel to see her again. My emotions are a maelstrom swirling through me, threatening to tear me apart on the spot. Anguish, fear, bitterness, empathy, determination, shame, wistfulness, uncertainty, contempt. They pummel me, too quick to recover before the next blow comes. I gasp, trying not to drown as they threaten to overwhelm me.

When the king says "Ghibellines," her mask drops. She stares at Floren's rulers with naked hatred. In a blink of an eye, the placid expression is back, but the shaken feeling lingers, letting me know I didn't imagine it.

All she cares about is revenge. Fury fills me. I cling to it, digging my nails in, refusing to let go. My vision narrows until all I see is Godmother Twelve. *The king and queen are innocent, but she doesn't care. She destroyed my life for nothing.* I clench the tray, yearning to fly across the room and tear her to pieces.

Godmother Twelve touches her bun, light flashing off the gold bracelet on her wrist. A knowing smile plays on her lips as she studies her glass, then sets it on the table beside her.

Time stops.

Godmother Twelve sits in her office behind the large desk, holding a small vial of clear liquid. Sunlight streams through the windows, creating a warm glow in the room as she lectures me on its uses. "All it takes is a drop. Odorless, tasteless. No symptoms to alert the victim to seek help. Two hours after they drink it, they'll die, making it impossible to trace the toxin back to the source."

The Godmothers poisoned the wine for the toast. Everyone here is going to die.

I can't get enough air. The king's speech is winding down. *I have to stop them.*

Need a plan, need a plan, need a plan. Screaming— would screaming work? No, I'd just get dragged back to the dungeon. Nobody would believe a traitor's warning.

My eyes fall on a decorative lamp in the wall niche. I dump the tray on the table, grab the lamp, and hurl it against the embroidered curtains with all my might.

The lamp shatters. Oil explodes across the wall. For a moment, the ballroom holds its breath, then screams erupt. Flames climb the curtains. Shouts. Another set of curtains bursts into flames. Glass shatters as everyone stampedes for the doors. The crowd at the door bottlenecks, increasing the panic. People pound on the windows, trying to break the thick glass.

The king and queen are surrounded by their guards and rushed out of the room through a hidden exit behind the dais. I follow them with my eyes, making sure they're safely gone, then turn to help with the fire. Servants, guards, and nobles run forward to put out the flames.

I was a little too efficient with my impromptu plan.

People dash around the ballroom, grabbing filled pitchers, glasses, and bowls to douse the flames. The air is heavy with smoke and ash. One guard staggers forward with an armful of staffs and pikes. The spontaneous fire brigade uses the long weapons to tear the curtains off the walls, then stomp the flames out. Scorch marks mar the wooden floor and plaster wall. The group moves to the next set of curtains, their faces determined.

Once it's clear the palace isn't in danger of burning down, I separate from the group, looking for an escape. I still need to find Gaia. The Godmothers won't stop at one attempt. They were thwarted this time, but they'll strike again. Soon.

Another volunteer steps to the side and swipes his arm across his forehead.

I gasp and back away, my steps clumsy.

Nicolas does a double take, then grasps my shoulders. His face is smudged with ashy streaks, his scorched scarlet shirt bearing the brunt of his battle with the fire. "What happened? Are you hurt?" His grip tightens. "What are you doing here? Gaia was going to smuggle you out through the tunnels. You can't be here."

"Nicolas." *He's safe. He's here.* My eyes tear up as I wrap my arms around him, making sure he doesn't disappear. "There's so much I have to tell you."

His arms tighten around me. "I'm sorry for yelling at you. It was cruel and inexcusable. I'll apologize fully later." He looks around. "Right now, we need to get you away before someone recognizes you and calls the guard. My parents are being completely unreasonable. We'll get this imposter nonsense figured out after everything calms down, but for now it's best you hide until I can talk some sense into them."

My heart sinks. "Gaia didn't tell you?"

Nicolas looks at me, his eyes concerned. "She said you're going to wait at the farm for us. Did something change?"

He still believes I'm Princess Aryanna. I want to blurt out the truth, tell him my real name, but I can't risk turning him against me now. There are higher stakes than my identity. *He can be furious with me later.* "There's no time. Serafina's trying to kill your family. We have to make sure your parents are safe."

I hold my breath. There's nothing to support my claim that a trusted family adviser he's known for years is plotting against his parents. It's ridiculous. I'm the girl who escaped from the dungeon and is rightfully accused of treachery. There's no reason for him to believe me.

He grabs my hand. "They'll be in their suite."

34

Running doesn't leave much room for talking, but I do my best to fill Nicolas in about the Godmothers between wheezes. He knows a little from what Gaia's told him over the years, but she's left a lot out. I skip over how we're both involved with the Godmothers for now—the important thing is to get everyone protection; then I can confess my crimes.

As long as he's safe.

The hallways grow lavish as we move deeper into the palace. Thick carpet muffles our pounding footsteps. Everyone is still in a state of disbelief and fear from the ballroom fire. The few guards we see are surrounded by frightened people and too far away to be of any use.

A fresh wave of energy fills me as we reach the last flight of stairs leading to the royal suite. I spring up the first step—then I'm yanked off my feet and dragged backward. An arm wraps around me from behind, trapping my arms to my sides. Cold steel presses against my neck.

Nicolas slides to stop and draws his knife. "Let her go." His voice is deadly, his eyes burning with promised pain.

Godmother Seven says, "You don't want to do that, boy. Think of the girl. You don't want her to get hurt, do you?"

"Throw it," I shout at him.

When he hesitates, I squirm, fighting to break her hold. She digs the knife in. Fire races across my skin. I bare my teeth, stretching my neck away from the blade's edge.

Nicolas lowers his weapon, his face twisted with pain. "Don't hurt her." His voice breaks on the last word.

"No, Nicolas! You have to stop her!"

The Godmother's breath is hot on the back of my neck. "Toss the knife, and any other weapons you have on you. She'll pay for it if you forget anything."

Nicolas moves slowly, his eyes trained on us. The blade hits the carpet with a dull thud, followed by a boot knife. Tears fill my eyes as Seven instructs him to walk in front of us. She pushes me along, using me as a shield, her iron grip stopping me from grabbing the dagger strapped to my thigh.

We turn down hallways, moving farther away from the royal suite and populated sections of the palace to the west wing near the storage rooms. The chill grows stronger with every step. Seven directs Nicolas down several unlit passages until our path ends in an undecorated room with several plain chairs.

Vivia is waiting inside.

Nicolas shouts a string of curses at her as Seven pulls me inside the room, the blade steady at my throat.

Vivia looks him over. "I see Aryanna told you about our organization. Good, that saves time." She points her cane at a chair.

The prince sits, every muscle quivering, the vein in his forehead pulsing. Seven moves me to stand in front of him while the other Godmother binds his arms and legs.

Nicolas gives me a tight smile. "Everything will be fine."

I sniffle. "Of course it will. I'm just upset I missed the ball. The food looked delicious."

Seven shifts the knife. "No talking."

After she ties the last knot, Vivia dusts off her hands. "Take her and find his little red-haired friend. She's in east wing. The girl knows where."

"I don't. I haven't seen her in days."

Seven says, "You never could lie properly. It's amazing they didn't discover you sooner." She presses the blade into my skin. "If you can't be of use to us, there's no need to keep you alive." Blood trickles down my neck as I suck in my breath.

Nicolas's strained voice breaks the silence. "Show her."

I force the word out around the lump in my throat. "No."

"Aryanna, look at me." His gray eyes are calm. "Dying here won't serve any purpose. Make your life count."

The fight drains out of me at his words. *He's right.* I can make a stand here, but it won't mean anything. It's only a matter of time before they find Lia. Every moment I stay alive is another chance to escape. Another opportunity to save Nicolas. And Lia, while I'm at it. "Fine."

Vivia sniffs. "At least you're not completely useless. I'll wait here for Serafina, then meet the others at the gate. We can toast our victory tonight."

"Make sure you stick to the plan." Seven drags me backward to the door.

He gives me a crooked smile. "Don't have too much fun without me."

"I'll be back soon," I vow, a tear sliding down my cheek.

One last look at Nicolas, then we're ripped apart.

As soon as we clear the room, Seven twists my arm up behind my back, keeping the knife pressed firmly against my side. Her hand grips me with bruising force. "Put your other hand on your neck. We're going to walk quickly to wherever you're hiding that guttersnipe. If you try to delay or lead me astray, you'll regret it."

And wish I was dead. It's tempting to lead her to another part of the palace, but if I deceive her and lose, Nicolas will suffer.

I cling to the hope that Vivia won't harm Nicolas before he's rescued. That he's too valuable as leverage. The Godmothers have always chosen subterfuge over a frontal assault; I just pray to the heavens they don't change their ways now.

Taking the long path to the kitchen buys me a few extra minutes. *There must be a way to stop Seven.* She didn't check me for weapons, either believing I couldn't get my hands on one or she's confident of her ability to disarm me if I attack. *Definitely the second option.* And she has every right to be. In all our years of training, I've never defeated her.

The weapons under my jacket are too hard to get in this position. If I can distract her for a moment and break free, or get the knife out of my thigh sheath, I might have a chance. Attracting someone's attention would work too. I could tell them what's happened after they take me away from Seven. *No—bad plan.* Seven would kill me first, claiming I was attacking her or trying to escape again. Nobody would know they've captured the prince. If Vivia senses she's about to be discovered, she's fully capable of killing Nicolas. I have to escape and get back to him.

Seven pulls me closer, concealing the knife at my back

as we pass the kitchen. It's quieted since I was here earlier. The aftermath of the interrupted ball is on full display. A few servers try to balance trays on surfaces already overflowing with glasses and stacks of plates. An army of dishwashers line up at the sinks, their elbows buried in suds. Nobody spares us a glance as we walk by the door and continue down the hallway.

The Godmother twists my arm harder, and I reflexively bend forward. My mind flashes back to the first time I was in the ballroom. *Nicolas's voice echoes around the empty room as he walks me through getting out of an arm lock. "The key is to surprise them and break their grip. Shift your weight unexpectedly and throw them off balance." He carefully bends my arm behind my back. "The first thing you do is ..."*

We turn the corner to Lia's room. My free elbow flies at Seven's face as I stomp on her foot. Lunging ahead, I punch forward, throwing all my weight in front of me. Seven's hold breaks. I twist around and shove her back.

It worked! Keeping my eyes trained on Seven, I grab two blades from the small collection of weapons under my jacket. "Lia! Margherita! Barricade the door." My arm tingles as the blood flows back into the muscles.

She lazily pulls out another knife as her lip twists. "I've been looking forward to this. You've been a burr on our heels for too long. Serafina was a fool for involving you."

I hold the weapons at the ready, staring down the Godmother. "You can't help yourself, can you? There's a lecture for everything. You spent more time talking than training me."

Seven sneers. "I knew you were a waste of my time. You're too simple to learn anything. Finally, I can rid myself of you."

My mind screams with the need to get back to Nicolas, but urgency will only get me killed faster. The narrow space and door at my back means there's no room to retreat, so every move has to count. *One deep breath. Two. Go!*

I spring forward. Steel clashes. *Keep her moving.* I twist away, avoiding her lower attack, then dart forward, slashing at her arm. *Keep her on the defensive.*

A kick aimed at her knee misses but carries me far enough forward to grab her wrist. A yank on her thumb forces her to drop the knife. I pin her other arm against the wall with mine. We wrestle, locked together.

She turns and shoves me down the hallway. My elbow bangs against the wall, sending shooting pain through my arm. I throw my knife. The blade whistles by her ear as she ducks to the side. Before she straightens, I have another knife in my hand, ready to attack.

I kick at her knee again, then sweep my leg. She anticipates, moving the same direction as my attack, her foot catching my kneecap with a loud crack. I fall to the floor. My knife barely blocks hers.

Seven hammers relentlessly, her blade flying through the air. Attack follows attack. I squirm along the floor, trying to get space to stand. Seven follows, seeking an opening in my defense. My arms shake. She slashes the sleeve of my coat, narrowly missing my arm.

I kick her chest, forcing her back. My legs are clumsy as I scramble to my knees, desperately trying to get up. Seven's hand snaps back to throw the knife. I fling my body to the side of the hall, cursing the small space. She won't miss.

Clank.

Seven crumples into a heap on the floor.

Lia leans against the wall, panting, a metal pitcher in her

hand. "I have no idea what Nicolas sees in you. I spend most of my time rescuing you from the disasters you drop on our doorstep."

I stare at her, dumbfounded. *She defeated Seven! She doesn't even have a proper weapon. Is it wrong to be jealous?*

"Are you going to lay there napping, or are you going to help me?" She slides along the wall, her hand pressed to her side.

I scramble up the rest of the way, catching myself as my injured knee buckles, then limp over. She leans on my shoulder, and together we stumble to the room. A terrified Margherita cowers on the far side of the space, hiding under a dusty brown blanket.

Lia settles into the corner with a groan. I snatch the blanket from Margherita and tear the bottom into long strips. After binding and gagging Seven, I drag her into the room and search her for weapons, passing her knives to Lia. My throbbing knee threatens to crumple more than once. I tear more strips and wrap it. It only needs to hold for another hour; after that, it won't matter.

I fix Lia with a steely glare. "Promise me you won't stab Seven unless she tries to escape or hurt you."

Lia snorts. "Seven? Seriously?" When I scowl, she widens her eyes and bats her lashes. "I would never hurt someone … even if they deserve it."

I put my hands on my hips.

"It's not like one or two little knife wounds will kill her. Look at these blades, they're puny! A splinter would cause more damage than these things."

"She needs to be interrogated." I shove Margherita outside over her weak protests, leaving Lia and the unconscious Godmother in the room. "Barricade the door this time. A half-grown kitten could overpower you. Don't trust anyone; they could work for the Godmothers." I slam the door behind me.

This ends now.

35

I force my steps to slow when I approach the room where I last saw Nicolas. As much as I'd like to burst inside, I need to be smart. Keeping low, I inch over to the doorway, listening for any movements inside. The only sounds are my heartbeats and harsh breathing. *There's only one way to find out if they're still here.*

I put one knife between my teeth and hold another ready as I grab the door handle. *One, two, three—go!*

The empty room brings a mix of relief and dread, until I see the body in the corner.

My legs collapse as pain rips through my chest. *Nonononono.* I gasp for air, tears streaming down my face. *Nonononono. It's not him, it can't be.* My clammy tunic sticks to my skin as I stare, unable to turn away from the horrific sight. It takes too long for my mind to register the size and clothing are wrong for Nicolas. *It's not him, it's not him.* The shaking won't leave me, even as I reassure myself over and over that it's not the prince.

I crawl over to the corner, loath to investigate, but

needing to know.

Vivia's sightless eyes stare at the wall.

Bile rushes up, burning my throat. *She'sdeadshe'sdeadshe'sdead.* I scurry to the far wall and press my palms to my head. Vivia may have been my enemy, but I never wanted this. *She was alive and now ... now she's ...*

Stop it. This won't help anyone. Nicolas and his parents are in danger. I squeeze my eyes shut and breathe slowly through my mouth, trying to rid my senses of the iron taint in the air. My mind finally quiets enough to think through what this means.

As much as I'd like to believe this means the prince was rescued, there's scant chance of that. The palace guards wouldn't leave a body for someone to stumble across, and they would watch the room to identify and ambush any conspirators. Or the prince would have people looking for me and waiting here in case I came back. No, Nicolas is still a prisoner.

Vivia was waiting for Godmother Twelve. Godmother Twelve or her helpers must have killed Vivia, then drugged Nicolas and taken him somewhere. I refuse to consider the alternative.

Think, think, think. Where would she take him? How could she best leverage him?

Her time is running out with my betrayal and the failed attempt in the ballroom. She won't risk leaving the prince alive, now that he knows about the Godmothers. She's dispatching her allies so she's not planning a retreat to regroup. Ransoming Nicolas is pointless. Same with using him as a hostage. *What can Nicolas give her right now that nothing else can?*

Access to King Luka and Queen Renata. With everyone on the alert because of the fire—and mayhap a missing prince—they'll be well protected. A couple of the Godmother's spies could carry Nicolas close to their rooms, then she can drag him into sight of the guards and call for help. As a trusted advisor and Council member who brought the prince to safety, she would be welcomed by the king and queen instead of turned away. Some of the burning guards might even be in her employment.

I don't know how she can murder the entire royal family without raising suspicions about her involvement, but I'm certain she has a plan to do so. Once they're killed, chaos will reign. The Godmothers could assassinate key nobility, and blame will fall on the person's political rivals as they all vie for the throne. The Godmothers will easily take control of the overwhelmed kingdom—whatever Godmothers are left alive, that is.

Surprised and scared looks follow me as I race to the king and queen's suite. People shout, demanding to hear what the new emergency is. I ignore the nobles but pause long enough with a few small groups of servants to order them to find Gaia. Nobody seems to recognize me before they run off to search.

When I reach the long hallway with the king and queen's rooms, I stop and catch my breath, sneaking a look around the corner. Eight guards are stationed outside the entrance.

Of course it can't be easy.

The wall cools my feverish skin as I lean back and stare at the ceiling. I use my sleeve to wipe the sweat rolling down my face. *They're not so incompetent as to let me waltz in there. If only I could climb the wall again—but I'm in no shape to make that trip and survive.*

There must be a way to trick the guards into telling me whether Nicolas and Godmother Twelve are inside. Best to be direct and ask for Lady Serafina so I draw less attention. Asking for Nicolas will only make them suspicious, especially if they're aware he's missing. The guard uniform might buy me a few moments of anonymity to get my answer and leave before they realize who I am. I'll have to trust to luck that they don't notice the damage from my earlier activities before I get my answers.

I swing my arms casually as I walk toward the guards, battling the urge to pull my knives. "I'm looking for Lady Serafina. Is she inside?"

The closest guard draws his sword. "It's the imposter!"

"How did she get out?"

"Attack!"

They run at me in an uncoordinated group.

Burn it. I grab two of the knives secured at my back and leap forward to meet them, catching them by surprise. If they had any idea how to fight in a group, they could overwhelm me in seconds. But their bumbling and interference with each other gives me a slim chance.

Everything is shape and shadow as I move on instinct, whirling and attacking too quick for thought. My mind only captures flashes of images.

Snarling at the guard trying to stab my foot.

A man reeling back, blood pouring from his nose.

Falling to the ground when one of them catches my bad knee.

Sinking my teeth into the arm of an assailant.

Dazed, I sway in the hallway, a lone knife in my shaking hand. *When did I lose the other one?* My arms drop to my side. The guards are on the ground around me, moaning or unconscious. It's hard to close the fingers on my left hand, but I don't feel any pain there. My limbs are full of rocks.

I stagger into the suite. My feet shuffle across the carpet. Godmother Twelve calls out cheerfully, "We're in here."

My grip tightens on the knife. I try to form a plan as I limp through the empty room—nothing. It's Godmother Twelve. She's already thought of everything. When I reach the green drawing room, I lean heavily against the doorway, taking the weight off my trembling knee as a coldness grows inside me.

The queen sits in the center of the room. Her body is limp, her eyes closed, head lolling against her chest. Godmother Twelve stands behind the queen's chair, a knife resting lightly in her hand.

The Godmother's eyebrows raise in surprise. "Aryanna. I thought you'd be dead by now. Seven's lost her edge."

I grasp the door jamb, my heart thundering as I look for Nicolas. *Where is he? He has to be here.* On the second pass, I spot him tucked under a blanket at the end of the couch. His chest rises and falls in an even pattern. *He's alive!* My body sags against the doorway, and I fumble the knife, nearly dropping it.

She makes a *tsk* noise as she takes in my appearance. "You look ghastly. It's hard to believe you're the same girl who dazzled the prince. Well, come inside. A princess shouldn't lurk in doorways, even one as pathetic as you. Not that you ever paid attention to etiquette." The knife taps against the queen's shoulder.

I stumble into the room. My exhausted muscles cry out. My chest hurts. Everything hurts. Only fear keeps me on my feet. "Don't you want to know if Seven is alive?"

"I can tell by your self-righteous tone she is. Pity.

Another loose end I'll have to tie up." The Godmother watches me with an impassive expression, seemingly no more interested than if I was discussing the weather over breakfast. "Get rid of your weapons." She waits while I toss the knife to the side. "Now the rest of them."

It's tempting to pretend I don't have any more, but the Godmother knows me well. Someone will discover the guards soon and raise the alarms. I need to play along until the queen and Nicolas are out of danger.

My shoulder refuses to twist far enough to reach the knives at my back. It takes several minutes of fumbling for my uncooperative hands to untie the band of fabric holding the blades and drop it to the floor.

Godmother Twelve shifts the knife closer to the queen's neck. "The king will join us shortly. He's dealing with some nuisance attacks on the outer wall by my allies. Then we'll take back Floren, and the Godmothers will be restored as its rightful rulers."

Even now, she lies. I shake my head. *It doesn't matter. Just keep her distracted so she doesn't realize the problem with her plan. It's only a matter of time until someone discovers the guards.* "Why? Why do all this?"

She looks past me toward the suite's entrance. "Because Floren deserves better."

I clench my fists. *More lies.* "You never needed me! Why couldn't you have left me alone?"

"Manners, child. I raised you better than that. But I suppose there's only so much you can do with ill breeding." She pats her hair. "I never leave things to fate. Why throw one knife and hope you hit your mark when you can throw twelve and guarantee you will? Relying on a single path to victory would be foolish. I made sure I would succeed, no matter the obstacle."

"That's all I am to you, a means to an end." My voice cracks. "You never cared about me. You tried to turn me into a monster." The hurt and pain come rushing in until all I want to do is scream. "But it didn't work. I know what you are. You're the monster, not me."

She glances at the ceiling and takes a deep breath, then brings her eyes back to me, a pained expression on her face. "You're wrong. I loved you like a daughter. It broke my heart when you betrayed me. I only wish you could see what they really are and be at my side when I defeat them." Her brow furrows, and she holds out a beseeching hand to me. "Won't you reconsider? Come back to me, and we can be a family again."

To my everlasting shame, a small part of me wants to believe her. I thought all those feelings were crushed out of me when I learned the truth about the Godmothers. "Nicolas and his parents have shown me what a true family is. I'll never trust your lies again."

"So dramatic, Aryanna. You never could grasp subtlety." She shrugs, her expression smoothing to indifference. "If you insist on betraying me, then you'll meet the same fate they do."

Better that than a knife in my back. "You can't kill them. Everyone will know it was you, and they'll execute you as a traitor. You'll never sit on the throne."

"Do you think so little of me?" A smile slowly grows on her lips. "Actually, you present me with an interesting opportunity. I was going to wait until the king returned and then poison the whole family. Myself too, though I would miraculously survive, of course. But now you've walked in here, leaving a path of destruction through the guards, proving how dangerous you are. Anyone harboring doubts will be thoroughly convinced of your treachery."

I wince.

"Imagine how devastated the king would be having his wife and son murdered by someone he invited into his home. How he'd despair that he left them behind where the imposter could find them. It would be quite enjoyable to watch him torture himself in the coming months. Wresting every night and day with how he might have saved them if only he'd stayed. I'll even let him comfort me when I weep about how I couldn't stop you in time."

The floor drops out from under me. *She's going to kill Nicolas and the queen, then blame me for it. The perfect patsy once again. She'll get away with everything.* A hollowness overtakes me. I can't even summon up any anger.

Her eyes gleam. "I can encourage him to take revenge on Cabriare or Linaria or whatever enemy I choose to blame. Then I'll sit back and watch as he destroys his kingdom in an unjust war before I finally end his misery. Oh yes, this is quite an enticing option." She gives a light laugh. "Ah, my dear. You've been so much more useful than I anticipated. It's good to know the years spent on you weren't wasted after all."

Stall, stall stall. Desperate, I hit her with the weapon that'll do the most damage. "Killing them won't bring your sister back."

Her face goes white. "Who told—what are—" Her control snaps back in place, and she flushes. "Thirteen. I thought that traitor perished years ago. No matter, I'll deal with her later. It will be a pleasure making her pay for her betrayal."

I'm out of time. Help isn't coming. I need to move, but my feet are rooted to the carpet.

Godmother Twelve yanks Queen Renata's head back, exposing the queen's throat. She holds up the knife. "If you have any last words, say them quickly."

My skin breaks out in a cold sweat. Nausea sweeps through me as my body trembles. *Nonononono.* I choke out, "Don't." My eyes dart to Nicolas, then back to his mother.

Her lip curls, her amber eyes filled with disgust. "Pathetic. This is why I never trusted you. You could never do what's necessary."

It's true. The Godmother knew it before I did.

But that doesn't make me weak.

Fire burns away the fear. I'll do whatever it takes to protect the people I love.

My vision narrows in on Godmother Twelve. This is the woman who lied to me my entire life. Killed my parents. Kidnapped me. Used me as a pawn in her personal war. Kept me in the dark, then threw me away when I figured out the truth. Turned me in for execution. She'll never stop hurting people. She needs to be stopped. *And I have one last trick up my sleeve.*

I keep my eyes locked on hers as I reach into my pocket, my hand closing on the dagger's hilt.

Time slows.

The Godmother's blade flashes in the light.

My knee buckles as I throw the knife. It curves as it slices through the air. The dagger drives into her chest. Godmother Twelve collapses, fingers clawing at the blade. Her pain-filled eyes lock on me, accusing me. Blood wells up between her hands. Her eyes glaze over. With a last gasp, she falls forward onto the carpet, then stills.

I stumble back, my hands out in front of me to ward off the sight. Cold spreads through my chest, freezing my lungs. *She's dead. She's dead. I didn't mean to! She's dead. She can't be dead.* The moment replays over and over, the knife flying through the air, the angle wrong. I drag my nails down my cheeks. *What have I done? She's dead. She's dead.* My arms wrap around my middle as a metal taste floods my mouth. *I destroy everything I touch. She didn't have to die.*

A terrible blackness threatens to overwhelm me. I push it down. *Not now. Don't think.* I clench my fists, focusing on the broken nails biting into my palms. Every breath gets my full attention. I carefully retrieve a knife from the floor, concentrating on its reassuring weight in my hand the texture of the hilt.

Time is running out. Any moment, the alarm will go up all over the palace. I have to get out of the suite before I'm discovered with the drugged royals and a dead Councilor.

I should be running for the door, but my heart pulls me to Nicolas. Kneeling next to the couch, I place my hand against his cheek, wishing I could say goodbye.

The prince stirs with a moan.

"Nicolas? Are you all right?"

His gray eyes open, blinking in the light. "Aryanna?"

What I wouldn't give to hear him call me Aurelia, if only one time. I force a smile. "I'm here. Did she hurt you? Did she make you eat or drink anything, or put anything on your skin?" *Please don't be poisoned, please don't be poisoned, please don't be poisoned.*

"She mixed something into a glass of wine. It was sweet. Like wild blueberries." He struggles to sit up, the tangled blanket and his clumsy movements hindering his progress.

I blow out a breath. "Sleeping draught. You'll be fine." I

tug at the covers, my movements just as blundering as his. He breaks free of the confinement with a triumphant, "Finally," then puts his hand to his head. "I feel terrible." His eyes widen at the sight of his mother slumped in the chair in the middle of the room. "What's going on? Where's my father."

"He's handling an attack on the city. She's fine, I think, just drugged, like you." I step aside so he can see Godmother Twelve on the floor, keeping my gaze averted from the grisly sight. "I don't know what she used, but the doctors should check for poisons just in case."

Nicolas swallows rapidly. "Burn it, Aryanna."

I lower my eyes. *He's right to be disgusted.* The Godmother's accusing look flashes across my vision; her gasps roar in my ears. I turn away from him, swallowing hard. *She's didn't deserve this. She didn't have to die.* I shrug weakly. "It was an accident."

He runs a hand down his face. "Let's get my mother somewhere safe, and then we can sort this mess out with my father."

Nicolas leans on my shoulder as he stands, his legs shaky. Mine aren't much better as we make our way across the room.

We've only managed a few steps when the suite's doors burst open. Shouts echo as the guards run through the rooms. Too late, help has finally arrived.

Before I can stop him, Nicolas calls, "In here."

Panic hits me. *I killed Godmother Twelve. I'm a traitor.* I press back against the wall. *They're here. They'll kill me. I need to escape.* Faced with death, I'm surprised by how much I want to live.

The first two guards in the room take one look at the

scene, then drop to one knee. Crossbow bolts slam into the wall next to me.

Nicolas yells, "Don't hurt her!" He moves between me and the men.

One of the guards runs to the queen and scoops her up, carrying her into a side room and out of sight. The rest ready their crossbows while another reaches a hand out to the prince. "Highness, come away."

Nicolas shields me with his body as I shrink against the wall. "I command you, stop."

The guards stare at me, death in their eyes.

They're too wrapped up in bloodlust to listen to him. I wrap my arm around Nicolas, my knife hovering near his throat. "Back up, back up. Clear the doorways. If anyone comes close, he's a dead man."

"What are you doing?"

I whisper, "Trust me."

And he does. Nicolas struggles in my grip, but it's only because of the awkward position. We both know he could easily break my weak hold.

One of the men shouts, "Do what she says."

The guards shuffle to the side a few steps, crossbows still pointed at us.

Idiots! One false twitch and they could kill their prince. I yell at the guards to drop their weapons, but to a man they refuse, compromising by lowering the crossbows to aim at our legs.

I try to twist us so my body will partially shield his, but Nicolas stubbornly shifts his weight in front of me. I hiss in his ear, "Turn sideways."

"Not on your life. Keep moving."

Between my threats and Nicolas's orders, the guards

back off enough to allow us to maneuver into the hallway.
Once the suite's doors close, they immediately start shouting
and pounding to get out.

Nicolas braces the doors until I can jam a nearby table
against them, temporarily locking the guards inside.

He says, "What now?"

"You stay here and let them out in ten minutes. Tell
them you overpowered me, but I managed to escape. That
I'm heading toward—" *What's the quickest way out of the
palace?* "—the southeast gate. Make sure the doctors see
your mother right away."

He grabs my hand. "You can't leave. They'll understand
after we explain about the Godmothers."

"There's no time. They'll kill me on sight." I shove him
over and sprint to the servants' stairway at the end of the
hall.

Nicolas follows on my heels. "I'll protect you until we
can explain everything. They won't hurt you."

He's too optimistic. I've escaped from the dungeon,
killed the beloved Councilor who rescued the prince, and
then taken the prince hostage. Not to mention they probably
think I poisoned the queen. Nothing will stop them. Every
second I'm in the palace is a heartbeat closer to my death.

The prince closes the gap. "Aryanna, tell me what
happened. What's really going on?"

My steps falter as the image of the knife in Godmother
Twelve's chest flickers across my mind. *Not now.* "Ask
Gaia."

Fire races across my arm. I cry out, tripping to a stop,
clamping my hand across the bleeding wound on my bicep.
A crossbow bolt is buried in the door in front of me.

Nicolas waves his arms at the advancing guards. "Halt."

Two bolts fly past him, narrowly missing us both.

They're going to kill us both!

I open the door to the servants' stairway, grab the back of his tunic, and yank him inside with me. As the door slams shut, the crossbolts pepper the other side with alarming thunks.

"Do you believe me now?"

I don't wait for an answer as I barrel down the stairs. We race through the palace, the guards falling behind. Nicolas follows my lead as we slide around corners and sprint through hallways. My knee screams at the abuse. It's too long before we fall through the doors into my former suite.

The prince puts his hands on his knees and gasps, "You can't stay here. This will be one of the first places they search. Hide in my room. Or the tunnel. Until I can explain."

"You saw the guards. They're out for blood. They won't bother trying to catch me alive." My bag is on the floor where I dropped it. My eyes dart to the window. "It doesn't matter. Even if they don't kill me, I'll end up back in the dungeon. I'm a fraud, like they said. I have to go." I hurry over and check the bag's contents. *Thank the heavens.* Everything I packed is still there.

"What are you saying? You have to tell them what you told me about the Godmothers. We'll figure everything else out after."

He doesn't understand, I've done everything they've accused me of. I'm an imposter who conspired with Floren's enemies and was planning to dethrone his family. I deserve to go back to the dungeon ... but not before I live.

He can't protect me from my crimes. I'm guilty. Once he learns the truth, he'll be forced to turn against me. To protect Floren and his family. And I won't blame him. I'll only be sorry that I hurt him and shattered his trust.

There's not enough time to make him understand before the guards come through the door. Nicolas will never let me leave, but I won't survive if I stay. He'll never forgive me for what I'm about to do, but it's just one more offense on an already long list of unforgivable acts. *It's the only way.*

Ignoring his pleas for an explanation, I dive into my closet. The small wooden chest is tucked into the corner. I dig through the contents, tossing bottles to the side until I find the five I'm looking for. Three go into my pockets, then I back out with the other two in my hands.

"You're right. I owe you an explanation. But we have to deal with a more urgent matter first." I shove the green bottle in his hands. "Drink this. I didn't want to scare you before, but that wine she gave you was poisoned. I recognized the taste you described. This is the antidote."

He pops the cork, then sniffs it. "It's not going to make me sick, is it?"

My stomach writhes. I laugh. "Don't worry, it's one of the better-tasting ones. Hurry up and drink the whole thing. The sooner you can counteract the poison, the fewer long-term effects it'll have."

"What about my mother?"

I hold up the yellow bottle. "This one is for her. Be glad you don't have to take it." I make a face.

He drinks the bottle's contents in one gulp, then smacks his lips. "You're right, not bad. Sweet."

I place the yellow bottle on the dressing table and add the three others in my pocket. I hastily write out the common names of the antidotes and instructions on their use. "These will help your mother if she's been poisoned, but you might need more. The apothecary in the city will have them in stock if the doctors don't." At the bottom, I add a list of other likely poisons, noting there could be more and that the Godmother was well traveled, so they shouldn't discount any exotic options.

Nicolas stares at the bottle in his hand, swaying on his feet. "It's sweet. Blueberries." He stumbles to me, his hands clutching at my shoulders. His eyes are unfocused. "Like the wine. Sleeping draught." The bottle drops to the carpet.

A hurt expression replaces the disbelief as he goes limp. The crossbow bolt wound on my arm burns as I grab his waist, supporting his weight so he doesn't injure himself on the way down to the floor.

He blinks rapidly, fighting to stay awake. "You …" His gray eyes slide closed and his breathing evens.

I brush a dark strand of hair away from his face, then gently rub my thumb across the line between his eyebrows until it smooths away, and his face looks peaceful.

My hand finds his. "You're safe now. Gaia will watch over you. I don't know if you'll ever find out the truth. But if you do, I—I hope someday you can forgive me." I clear my throat, forcing the lump down. "I want you to know, you saved me. I was trapped in darkness, but you led me into the light. You showed me what it means to have a real family. That I could have hopes and dreams, and I could … love someone. Love you. That's a debt I can never repay."

I drop my eyes and rub the fabric of his sleeve between my fingers. "You'll never see me again. It's what has to happen. My love will always belong to you, but someday you'll meet someone who replaces me in your heart. She won't have my fighting skills or sarcasm, but you'll love her anyway. Don't fight it when it happens. Let me go. She doesn't deserve to be compared to a fantasy. You'll have a long, joyful life with her. It's what I want for you. For Floren." Teardrops stain the fabric of his shirt.

I long to kiss him one last time, but I can't. I don't deserve it. I've betrayed his trust; I won't steal anything else from him.

I've stayed too long. I hold the back of his hand to my cheek for a moment, then force myself to turn away, wiping the tears from my cheeks. "Goodbye."

Gaia appears in the suite's doorway as I fling open the balcony doors. "Aurelia, wait!"

Heavy footsteps pound down the hallway toward my room.

"Take care of him. All of them." I disappear over the side.

36

I dangle my feet over the rock's edge, enjoying the way the light sparkles off the water, the tangy salt air deliciously different from the dry farmlands where I grew up. The endless blue sea stretches out before me. No matter how long I stay here, I don't think I'll ever tire of this view. Today the water is in a peaceful mood, the spray from the waves only reaching halfway up my perch. The sun pours warmth into my skin, making me boneless.

The city is everything I hoped and more. Here, I'm never alone. People flock to the sea to be inspired, trade, find love, or find themselves. Being an outsider doesn't draw any attention. It's easy to lose myself wandering the streets and watching people go about their days. I'll move on again soon, but it's home enough for now.

Time has let me heal. I'll forever carry the scars with me, but the pain has faded. For the first time I can remember, I've found moments of peace. I know Nicolas and his family are safe. With Serafina dead, the other Godmothers will retreat and lick their wounds, giving Gaia time to root them out.

I'll always be sorry I ended Godmother Twelve's life, but it was an accident. A little piece of me mourns who I thought she was before I came to the palace and learned the truth. A larger part is angry she ruined so many lives. That I never had a childhood because of her. That I'll never know my parents except through secondhand stories. Rage at the waste and pain threatens to take me over, but I do my best to accept it and move past it. Every day is a new battle. Some days it's easier to triumph than others.

My heart yearns to return to Floren, to see Nicolas again and explain everything. To beg his forgiveness. See what new delights they've introduced to the marketplace. But I settle for knowing the kingdom is protected. That Nicolas is out of danger. He'll have a happy life and I can cherish every memory of our time together.

Visiting the market here makes me feel close to him. I can imagine how he'd spend hours debating with the tinkerer about the best way to repair an item or try to charm a free sweet from the vendor before buying the entire tray and passing them out to the children. How we could spend hours admiring every weapon but agree our favorite merchant in Floren is still the best knifemaker in the world.

The wind ruffles my hair. I run my hand through it to untangle the strands, still surprised when it ends at my shoulders. I won't feel completely myself until it grows back to waist length.

"Lovely," Nicolas says from behind me.

I press my palms against the stone. A thousand emotions race through me: joy, fear, anger, pain, suspicion, happiness, confusion. "How did you find me?" My voice is impressively steady, given the turmoil inside.

"You didn't make it easy. It took all the resources Gaia and I have to trace your path over the past months. We missed you in Marseine by a few days. She's in the carriage, by the way. She insisted on coming."

He sits next to me on the warm rock, gazing out at the water. "We waited for you at the farmhouse. When you didn't come, we searched the villa."

Gaia told him. About my role in the Godmothers' plans. Why I was sent to Floren.

"You should have told me." His voice is soft.

I swallow past the lump in my throat. "I couldn't." He would've hated me. Never trusted me. And then, when he would have believed me, it was too late. Because I loved him. I couldn't hurt him, couldn't stand it if he rejected me. I'm always too late.

At least now I can get the answer to one question that's plagued me since I left Floren. "How is your mother?"

"Fine. She wasn't poisoned. Mostly she's angry at herself for being deceived all these years. We all are."

And I was a large part of that deception. Everyone in Floren must be horrified at how close Godmother Twelve came to succeeding. The Council is surely screaming for heads to roll.

The silence stretches as we watch the water lapping against the rocks.

I break first. "What are you going to do?"

"Take you back to Floren."

I nod. The words don't hold any surprise. I've committed too many crimes to disappear. Know too many secrets. If it wasn't Floren, it would be one of the Godmothers delivering their vengeance. I've lived my borrowed time to the fullest. There would always be one more thing to do or see, but I've relished every adventure since I left Floren.

"Please know I'm truly sorry. I'll go quietly. I won't fight or run away."

He tilts his face toward the sun. "You make it sound like I'm dragging you back to the dungeon."

"Aren't you?"

He finally looks at me, his gray eyes not giving anything away. "I should, after all the trouble you've put me through. Lying to everyone. Posing as Princess Aryanna. Assaulting half the guards. Drugging me, then leaving. The palace was in an uproar for weeks. It's a good thing Gaia was there to explain everything."

I add guiltily, "I set the ballroom curtains on fire too."

He runs a hand over his face as he groans. "I should have guessed. The heavens only know what you'll do when you come back. Next time, tell me about any assassination attempts before you take hostages or set the palace ablaze."

A warmth blossoms in my chest. "They seemed like good ideas at the time."

He yanks on his dark hair, leaving it adorably ruffled. "They were terrible ideas! You leave a path of destruction everywhere you go."

"Then why take me back?"

He pulls me into his lap. "Because I can't spend another day without you."

And then he kisses me.

Our first kiss was tender and passionate. Comparing that kiss to this one is like comparing a spark to a bonfire. Every brush of his hand ignites my love for him. Every heartbeat tells me I'm for him and he's for me. That same tug in my chest pulls me to him. Nicolas is the only man who will ever make me feel this reckless, this safe, like I've finally come home. He loves me for who I am, flaws and all. The world can crumble around us, but as long as we're together, we have everything. Our destinies are bound together.

He tucks a short strand of hair behind my ear, his gray eyes shining with passion and tenderness. "Aurelia. My love. Could you be happy in Floren? Happy with me?"

Tears fill my eyes. *He said my name—my* real *name. Just like I've dreamed about.* "Are you sure you want me? After all I've done, all the hurt I caused you … how can you ever forgive me? Or trust me again?"

"After Gaia told me everything, I won't deny that I was furious. But then I realized what you'd really done. How you saw through a lifetime of their lies and chose to help us, instead of the people you thought of as family. I can't imagine how difficult that decision was. I can only thank the heavens every day you were strong enough to make it and that you survived despite the danger it put you in. You saved us all."

I blush at the admiration in his voice, but I can't ignore the worry worming its way through my mind. "If this is your way of thanking me, you don't owe me anything. I did what I thought was right. What anybody would do. Now that I'm free of the Godmothers, I can live my life. And you can live yours."

His eyes sadden. "You don't wish to return to Floren? Or is it me? I swear, I would never force my affection on you. If it's what you want, I'll leave now and never bother you again."

"The heavens, no!" The idea that I would reject Nicolas is so ridiculous, it never crossed my mind he might feel vulnerable too. *How can I explain?* "I played a part. In

Floren, in my entire life, really. Princess Aryanna. I can't be her anymore. You deserve to fall in love with a real person, not an imposter who doesn't know who she is. Right now, I'm just a paper doll that doesn't exist."

He gently brushes a tear off my cheek. "Do you really think I don't know you? That I can't love you for who you are? Whether people call you Aryanna or Aurelia, it doesn't matter one whit. The real you will always shine through. You're the woman who charges at the battle when others would run away. The woman who can't resist a wager. Who looks to the heart of things when everyone is trying to lead her astray. Whose kindness shines through whether she's talking to a noble or a servant. There's a thousand moments and feelings and thoughts that are yours and yours alone, and that's who I love. That's who has my trust. From the moment you swung that stick at my head, my heart was lost. But I'll wait until the stars fall into your wild sea if you need time to discover who that is for yourself. My love will be here waiting when you're ready."

For a moment, all I can do is stare dumbfounded at him. Then I throw myself into his arms and kiss him, pouring all my love into our connection.

He breaks away with a laugh. "Is that a yes? You'll marry me?"

"Yes! Yes, yes, yes!" I kiss him again.

We walk along the shore hand in hand. Nicolas tells me of the events that transpired after I left the palace and the efforts they're making to find the remaining Godmothers. Godmother Twelve's plan to blame Cabriare for the murders at the ball, painting me as the culprit to start a war. How they uncovered her secret alliance with the Linarians. The other ways she planned to use me if her first plan didn't work out.

His face darkens. "It still gives me nightmares when I think about it. If she wasn't already dead …" He shakes his head, fists clenched.

Nicolas claims his parents understand why I did everything and smoothed over my return to Floren with the Council. Not everyone was happy about it. But with the evidence against Godmother Twelve they found at the villa, and the confirmation of my lineage, the king and queen were able to convince them to accept me. Not exactly a ringing endorsement, but better than I could have imagined. He says if anyone asks me about what happened at the palace that night, I should respond with "I'm sworn to silence." I'm fairly certain he made that last part up just to have a laugh.

Someday soon I'll tell him about my life at the villa and my travels after Floren, but right now I want to bask in the moment. It's hard to believe he's really here. That he's not a dream that will fade away at any moment. Every few minutes I squeeze his hand to make sure he hasn't disappeared. He feels the same, judging by how often he runs his hand down my hair or kisses my palm.

He pulls me to a stop and takes a bundle of fabric out of his coat. "I almost forgot."

Inside is the sapphire dagger. I bite the inside of my cheek. *My beautiful present.* The perfect gift from Nicolas. It meant so much to me. But I'll never be able to look at it without remembering Godmother Twelve. Another thing taken from me.

He puts an arm around my shoulder as I stare down at the weapon. "I wasn't sure if you would want it after … everything. Regardless, I'm buying you a new one. I need to make sure you don't run off with that weapons dealer."

I sniff back the tears threatening to spill. "Don't tempt

me. I'd have the best-outfitted armory in the world. Imagine all the havoc I could cause." I tuck the dagger back inside his coat. Tomorrow is soon enough to deal with the knife and all the emotions tied to it. Today is about happiness and enjoying the moment.

Nicolas covers his eyes. "I can, that's the problem. I promise, your weapon collection will be the envy of the kingdom. Just don't use it on the guards."

"I'm glad you brought that up." I take his hand and we continue our walk down the beach. "When I get back, I'm taking over your guard training. Somebody needs to keep you safe, and they're clearly not up to the task."

"Captain Rossi might object. He's a bit irked after your last confrontation with his men."

"Exactly my point. If one injured girl can defeat eight guards in hand-to-hand combat with two tiny little knives and outrun a squad firing crossbow bolts at her, not to mention break into the royal suite twice and kidnap the prince, consider what a real assassin could do. Someone needs to train them properly, and that someone is me. I'll have Lia help. It'll give her the opportunity to stab someone else besides me."

He chuckles. "I hope she takes you up on it once the doctors clear her, but it might be a while. She tries to knife anybody who comes near her. Makes it hard to see how well she's healing."

"I'm not worried. She's too irritating to die. She'd fight off the angels if they came for her."

"That she would. But it's not necessary in this case. The doctors agree she'll be back to her normal, cheery self in another month. Less if she stops trying to sneak out of bed every chance she gets."

"Have you tried tying her to the bedposts?"

"Chewed through the ropes. Twice." His eyes light up as we reach a group of low rocks. "Whoa-ho! Ware the rocks, milady. I must protect your delicate feet once again."

I laugh as he sweeps me into his arms and carries me over the small cluster. He gently sets me down in the sand, keeping his arm around my waist as I lean against his side. The sea breeze gently wraps around us as the water laps at our feet. The gentle roar of the waves lulls me into a living daydream.

As the sun sets, he reluctantly looks back. "Gaia wants to see you. She's been corresponding with your family. Your aunt and uncle are eager to meet you."

I stare at the water, wrapping my arms around my middle. "I don't want to see them." *What will they think of me?* The more I've learned about the king and queen of Cabriare, the more intimidating they've become. They can't possibly be happy to have a traitor as part of their family. "It's better if I stay away."

He gathers me into his arms. "My heart, you have nothing to be ashamed of. Besides, you're engaged to the prince of Floren. Your aunt and uncle will be thrilled when they find out. I hear he's quite the charmer."

I arch an eyebrow at him. "I've heard he's exasperating. Likes to stalk defenseless princesses in the woods for fun."

"There's nothing defenseless about a princess who draws a knife at every opportunity."

"We make quite the pair. I guess we deserve each other."

"The heavens help Floren when we're married. I'll have to double the size of the fire brigade and set triple watches on the palace walls."

"I promise to do my best to stay out of trouble. At least,

most of the time. A girl has to have a little fun now and then." I loop my arms around his neck. "And you still owe me five more wagers. I plan to collect each and every one of them from you."

He rests his forehead against mine. "It will be my pleasure."

***

Note from the Author: Word of mouth is crucial for any new author. If you enjoyed the book, please leave a review on Amazon, Goodreads, or your favorite review site. Even a few words make a huge difference and are greatly appreciated!

Thank You!
Amanda Kaye

Want more adventures with Aurelia and Nicolas?
Sign up to my newsletter to get an exclusive bonus scene from Nicolas's point of view and a novelette taking place after Aurelia returns to Floren:
https://www.amandakayebooks.com/briars-blades-subscribe/

ALSO BY AMANDA KAYE

To hear about the next exciting release from Amanda Kaye,
sign up for her newsletter at:
AmandaKayeBooks.com/subscribe-now/

<u>Blades Series</u>

Cinders & Blades (short story)

Briars & Blades

Wolves & Blades

Beasts & Blades

Sirens & Blades

Trails & Blades

<u>Other Short Stories</u>

An Oath of Fire

Slithers & Swords

Restless Tides

ABOUT THE AUTHOR

Amanda Kaye loves plotting new ways to torture her characters and throw them into danger. Nothing makes her happier than reading an amazing book with an awesome character arc; her favorite authors include Mercedes Lackey, Robin McKinley, and Patricia Briggs. She can always find an excuse to buy sparkly nail polishes and chocolate chip cupcakes. Amanda lives in sunny California with her two mini-monsters masquerading as kittens.

Her stories remind you that there's always a silver lining no matter how dark the night. She'd love to chat with you about your favorite books at:
www.amandakayebooks.com/subscribe-now/